TRUE COLOURS

When Kim inherits a seaside art gallery from her godfather, she unexpectedly decides to take it on — despite knowing next to nothing about art! Her new venture leads her to encounter the sophisticated art dealer, Mark, who proves both surprisingly helpful — and surprisingly desirable . . . But Kim is thrown off-kilter by the sudden appearance of a former boyfriend, and Mark is overshadowed by dark memories of his first wife. Will the pair succeed in conquering their trepidations, and finally reveal their true colours?

WENDY KREMER

$$\diamond$$

TRUE
COLOURS

Complete and Unabridged

LINFORD
Leicester

First published in Great Britain

First Linford Edition
published 2015

A catalogue record for this book is available
from the British Library.

ISBN 978–1–4448–2335–6

Published by
F. A. Thorpe (Publishing)
Anstey, Leicestershire

Set by Words & Graphics Ltd.
Anstey, Leicestershire
Printed and bound in Great Britain by
T. J. International Ltd., Padstow, Cornwall

This book is printed on acid-free paper

1

The vicar's surplice and the pages of his Bible rippled in the wind. Kim thought she recognized two of the people standing opposite, but couldn't remember where she'd seen them before. One other person in the small crowd caught her attention because of his stature and good looks. The wind dishevelled his hair and rumpled the dark scarf round his neck. Their eyes met for a moment and she looked down in haste. She concentrated on the petals of the roses on top of the simple coffin. Finally, the company murmured the Lord's Prayer, and people began to disperse.

She and her parents shook hands with the vicar, and then stood for a moment at the graveside. The people attending slipped away in ones and twos. Her father had planned to issue a verbal invitation to join them for something to eat and drink, but it was too late now.

They left and the church gate clanged loudly as her father shut it. 'It looks like we don't need to play hosts, so let's visit Bill's lawyer instead. He asked us to call if we had time. He wants to tell us about Bill's will. I already know what's in it. Bill told me what he intended to do years ago.'

Kim said, 'That's a good idea, Dad. It'll save you coming back another day.'

They wandered down the road leading to the village with its higgledy-piggledy assortment of dwellings. They found the lawyer's office quite easily. It was next to the main road, opposite a small half-timbered building housing a charity shop. They went inside and introduced themselves to his secretary.

★   ★   ★

A short time later, Kim eyed her parents across the small table in the cafe. 'You knew, and didn't try to stop him? I'm a book-keeper. I know nothing about art. I can't possibly do it.'

Her father nodded. 'He was adamant. You were his goddaughter. He wanted you to have it. He knew that your mother and I wouldn't take it on at our age. I told him so when he suggested it. He also knew that Shelley would never give up her top-notch job, or Roger his bookshop. He was counting on you. If you say no, the gallery and the cottage will be auctioned off and the proceeds go to a couple of local charities.'

'Perhaps that'd be better. I've a well-paid job that I like, a flat, and friends who live close by. I'd have to ditch everything and move here to take over a business I know nothing about.'

Her mother said gently, 'That's true, love, but it would be your own business. Think about the cottage. It's gorgeous. Bill looked after it and the garden so well. The village and the surrounding countryside are really lovely. People come here for their holidays.' She paused. 'With your qualifications you can always find another job if it doesn't work out.'

Kim sighed. 'Oh, why did he do it?'

Mr. Spenser gave his daughter a quick smile and his bushy eyebrows lifted. 'That's simple; he wanted you to have it.'

'But I know nothing about art. It's a very specialized area. It's not like running a bookshop or a pub. If you're enthusiastic and determined, you could cope. Why didn't he warn me? I'd have tried to talk him out of it.'

'Perhaps he was waiting for the right moment. I'm sure he didn't expect to die so suddenly. I'm positive he thought you would manage. Otherwise, he wouldn't have left it to you.'

'Whenever we visited him, we spent our holidays on nearby beaches or going to tourist attractions. I never spent any time in the gallery.'

'Sleep on it! Think about the pros and cons. Follow your instincts.' Mrs.

Spenser leaned forward. 'Like to look around the gallery and the house before we leave? I expect the lawyer has the keys.'

Kim looked at her watch. 'No. We won't get home before midnight if we stay much longer.'

They walked to the car park near the harbour wall. She noticed the man from the funeral service driving past them in a green Volvo. He looked their way and nodded briefly.

★　★　★

Howard was asleep when Kim got home. He'd emptied the fridge of food and created his usual chaos. There were towels on the floor, and socks and T-shirts were strewn wherever he had dropped them.

Kim was fed up. The men she chose always turned out to be completely insensitive and self-centred. She wondered if romantic, everlasting love really existed anymore. Men only seemed to have one aim — to get their girlfriends into bed. As she didn't believe in casual sex, her boyfriends never lasted long, and they told her she was hopelessly old-fashioned. Howard hadn't so far tried to get her between the sheets, but it was only a matter of time. He was no different to others. Admittedly, he could be charming and fun, but only when he made the effort. That was why she'd liked him in the beginning.

He now assumed he'd made a conquest, but he hadn't. She'd allowed him to stay overnight once a few weeks ago when his rugby team were playing locally. After that, he thought he could turn up whenever he liked. Even though he slept on the couch, the situation was aggravating. His obsession with rugby, his untidiness and his bogus buoyancy were driving her mad.

She didn't like being hurtful, but she definitely didn't want him as a permanent fixture in her life. It was better for him to understand that as soon as possible. She vowed not to get involved with any man from now on unless she felt that there was something very special about him.

When she left for work next morning, Howard was sprawled among tangled blankets on the living-room couch. He mumbled his hello and goodbye without opening his eyes.

★   ★   ★

Kim mutinied after work and didn't go to the local supermarket for a much-needed supply of fresh groceries. Howard sensed angry clouds were gathering. On her return, he insisted on taking her out for a meal. She hoped it wouldn't be like last time, when he'd forgotten his wallet and she had to pay.

They sipped their drinks and she considered his good-looking face. Howard had laughing eyes, floppy brown hair and most of the time he was easy-going and entertaining. Her problem was that she didn't love him. During a break in the conversation, she told him about her godfather's will.

'I've inherited his cottage and gallery, if I want them.'

His eyes widened. 'Wow! Fancy that! Didn't he have any children? Where did you say it was?'

'He was my father's cousin. He never married. It's a small seaside resort in Dorset, not far from Lulworth.'

Howard took a generous gulp of his beer. 'Gosh! It's like winning the lottery.'

Irritated, she said, 'I haven't decided if I'll accept yet. I know nothing about buying or selling art.'

'You'd be a fool to turn it down. You have a chance to escape the rat race and enjoy life for a while. You're a qualified book-keeper. You'll pick up the rest as you go along.'

'Howard! A book-keeper needs a business, but a successful business needs more than a book-keeper.'

'Aw come on, it's probably a little goldmine. If not, it's a breather from the daily grind, and a new experience. You'll find another job easily if it's a complete disaster.'

'You make it sound so simple.'

'Course it is. I'll come with you if you like. Two can live as cheap as one. I'd love a change of scenery.'

His words stunned her for a moment. Kim swallowed hard. The landlady brought their meal. It gave her a chance to conceal her reaction. Howard continued to elaborate about what a wonderful chance it was. Was he excited for her sake, or because he wanted her to include him in her future plans? It was high time she told him they'd come to the parting of the ways.

★　★　★

Next day Howard was playing against the local rugby team. Kim came home after shopping with a friend. The flat was empty but it was in a chaotic state. Howard's scattered and discarded clothes were everywhere. The kitchen table was covered with abandoned breakfast dishes, and a heap of dirty sportswear waited on the washing machine in the bath-room. He'd been searching for something, because several drawers were hanging out and some of the contents were on the floor. She viewed the tangled mess with mounting anger.

The telephone rang. Kim was smouldering inside when she saw her sister's number on the display. 'Hi, Shelley.'

'Hi, sis! Mum just told me about your inheritance. You're not seriously thinking about accepting, are you?'

She answered snappily, 'Why not?'

'I'm not suggesting you're not good at your job — you probably are — but you need skill to run an art gallery.'

Already exasperated and angry as she studied the state of the living room, Kim retorted, 'I know that, but not every business owner has a degree in management.'

'It's a pity that they don't. It'd mean fewer bankruptcies. Do you have an idea what the annual turnover of this place is? Does it have other assets or liabilities? Does it have any hidden debts, or a mortgage of some kind? If you take it on you should put your personal assets on a different footing. You could end up in debtor's prison for company commitments. Did he run the place on his own? If not, you may have to pay former employees some kind of compensation if you discharge them.'

Listening to Shelley was depressing. She was so rational and level-headed. 'What personal assets are we talking about?' Kim asked her.

'Your car, your furniture, that horrible-looking but valuable jewellery that Gran left you, and any savings. They're assets, and they'll vanish if you don't protect them.'

'Shelley, stop needling me. I haven't decided anything yet.' Looking at the disorder, she went on, 'I'm going down there now to take a closer look at the place.'

'If I had time I'd come with you, but we're giving a dinner party this evening for some important clients. I can't dodge it.'

11

Kim mused how far Shelley had wandered from her roots. Shelley's multi-course dinner parties with preceding cocktails would have scared her mother to death. 'Never mind! I'd rather be on my own. I won't do anything silly, promise.'

'I hope not. I want to hear all about it, so phone me on Monday. Not before seven.'

'Um, okay. How's Roger?'

'Fine. He's just gone out for a run while I figure out this evening's place-settings.'

Kim wondered if Roger was just trying to escape the fuss. She liked her brother-in-law. He owned a cosy bookshop. She often wondered what had attracted Shelley and Roger to each other in the first place. They were very different personalities. 'Give him my love.'

'Will do. I have to ring the catering company now to jog their memories, and then I'm off to the gym for a workout.'

'Rather you than me! I'll phone at the beginning of the week.'

* * *

As soon as Kim replaced the receiver, she mused that Howard had assumed she'd take on the gallery, and Shelley had assumed she wouldn't. Everyone, apart from herself, seemed to know all the answers. She marched to her bedroom and pulled a small overnight case from the bottom of the wardrobe. Looking around, she resisted an urge to clear the mess. She'd had enough. On her return, she'd ask him for the key. Howard was definitely not Mr. Right and it was time that she told him so.

She packed quickly. Ten minutes later, she was on the motorway and she began to relax. She'd make a decision this weekend.

* * *

The village pub had a couple of furnished rooms. They were clean and quiet. Kim signed in and went for a walk around the harbour before the

13

weakening sun disappeared for the day. The quay was empty and silent except for the soft hissing of the rising tide brushing the rough stonework, and the sound of the boats moving in their moorings against the harbour walls. Kim liked the tranquillity. The only people she noticed were a young couple out walking their dog.

Next morning, straight after breakfast, fresh breezes were blowing land-inwards from the water. Shoving her hands into the pocket of her windbreaker, Kim looked along the main road as it scrambled up the hillside. The church tower stretched towards the cloudy sky but the main body of the church was out of sight behind the high hedge bordering the lane. It'd be the perfect place to sit and think things over. As Kim walked up the road, she breathed the salty air and the sunned grasses growing along the verge. The lychgate squeaked as she pushed it open and went into the silent churchyard. Apart from the wind rustling the leaves on the gnarled trees, and the song of some hardy birds in the surrounding hedges, it was very peaceful. There was always a soothing atmosphere of stability and permanence in old churchyards, and this one was no exception. She retraced the way to Uncle Bill's grave and looked at the bare mound of earth topped with the fading flowers. Whatever else she did, she'd arrange for a headstone to be put up as soon as possible. She recalled happy days and loving memories with a cheerful, optimistic man.

The wind blew strands of her rust-brown hair across her pale cheeks and she pushed them aside. She saw a weather-worn bench alongside the wall. It was in a sheltered position facing away from the sea winds, and it overlooked the village. She went there to sit down. She pulled up her collar and leaned forward to gaze at the gorse growing on the neighbouring hillside.

'Miss Spenser?'

The deep voice made her jump. The man stood with his back to the sun, and Kim jumped to her feet. He was a tall, dark silhouette. She shifted her position so that she could see his face. He was the stranger she'd seen at Uncle Bill's funeral. He had a strong jaw; thick, dark hair; curved eyebrows and high cheekbones. Kim had to look up because he was at least a head taller. His face mirrored his confidence. There was no hesitation in his manner.

'Yes. And you are — ?'

He held out his hand. 'Mark Fraser. I hope I didn't scare you.'

She shook it. It was firm and warm. 'You did a bit. I thought I was alone.'

'Sorry, that wasn't my intention. I noticed you were coming here and I followed you. Wilson the solicitor told me you're Bill's sole beneficiary.'

'Yes, I am. You knew Uncle Bill?'

'I wasn't a close friend, but we respected each other. I liked him.' He paused. 'We were in the same business. In a sense we were rivals.'

'Oh.' Her youthful expression steadied. 'He never mentioned your name, but I know nothing about the business side of his life.' She studied his dark green eyes. She noticed he was also silently sizing her up.

'That's why I'm glad I have the chance to meet you. I intended to ask Don Wilson to pass on my offer, but this is better. I can do it personally and save time.'

'Your offer? For what?'

'Bill's business, with or without the cottage. I'd like another outlet and Bill's gallery has potential, even if the general economic situation isn't good at present.'

Startled, she replied, 'I haven't made up my mind what I'm going to do yet, Mr. Fraser. That's why I came back.'

His eyebrows lifted. 'You're not seriously thinking about keeping it?'

Stiffening, she said, 'Why not? Why shouldn't I?'

He thrust his hands into the pockets of his soft leather jacket. 'Because you haven't a clue how to run it, and probably no idea about art either.'

She resented his arrogance, even if it

was the truth. He was clearly the kind of man who didn't waste time in beating about the bush. He automatically assumed he knew all the facts. He was the sort of domineering wise guy she'd met before, at managerial level. 'You can learn all kinds of skill and knowledge if you're determined enough.'

He laughed abruptly. 'Knowing what to do or what not to do in the art world is more complicated than learning a new software programme or balancing the monthly ledgers. It's a matter of instinct.'

Either his use of vocabulary was coincidental, or he'd already checked Kim's background. 'That may be true,' she said, 'but perhaps I have those instincts. Perhaps I should give it a try. Uncle Bill hoped I would.'

'It would be a waste of your time. If you sell it to me, you can forget your worries and enjoy the money. I assure you that I'll pay the going price.'

Kim straightened and managed to answer through stiff lips, 'Mr. Fraser, I only inherited it recently. I intend to think carefully about the pros and cons before I decide anything.'

His jaw clenched and his eyes narrowed slightly. 'There aren't many pros from your viewpoint. You're a newcomer, the gallery isn't paying its way, you know nothing about art, and you haven't much time to learn. I can't judge if you have any of your godfather's instincts, but I doubt it.'

Bristling, she met his eyes without flinching. 'I think you take too much for granted. You shouldn't underestimate someone's determination, or what will-power can achieve. You're crossing your bridges before you come to them. Thank you for your offer; I'll give it due thought and let you know.' She remembered the terms of the will and added, 'I don't think I could sell it to you, even if I wanted to. If I refuse, the lawyer has to sell it to the highest bidder and give the money to a couple of local charities.'

He was silent for a moment and

continued to study her. Then he took his wallet from an inner pocket and extracted a visiting card. He held it out to her.

She took his card gingerly and avoided any contact with his fingers. She noticed a flash of amusement in his eyes, but it was very short-lived. She had to admit he was very attractive and had a delicious-looking mouth. What an annoying, overconfident, condescending and assertive man. He thought it was a foregone conclusion she'd jump at his offer. With a nod, she turned away quickly. He'd shattered the peace and quiet. If he was around, there was no point in staying here.

She stuffed his card into the pocket of her jacket and hurried towards the gateway. She didn't hear his farewell, nor did she think of saying goodbye herself.

2

Feeling unnerved, Kim walked back to the village, passing some of the typical whitewashed stone houses crowded closely together as she went. Her godfather's cottage and adjoining art gallery were on one of the bends. The cottage garden was full of late-blooming flowers in a multitude of colours. There was also an inviting bench in a sunny position alongside a wall.

She went to the gallery. To her surprise, it was open. Seascapes, land-scapes and a couple of framed aquarelle paintings were displayed in the bow windows. The woodwork was bright blue and the windows were clean and shiny. She lifted the old fashioned catch and a bell tinkled. The room was empty and her shoes echoed on the wooden planking. She heard faint movements from a rear room. She looked at the pictures on the walls. They were much the same as the ones in the windows.

'Good morning. Can I help you?' A smart-looking woman in late middle age, somewhat plump, with intelligent eyes and curly greying hair came towards her.

Kim smiled. 'I expect so. My name's Kim Spenser.'

The woman smiled and held out her hand. 'I thought it was you, but I didn't like to jump the gun. I haven't seen you for several years.'

She nodded. 'Once I started working if I visited Uncle Bill it was only for the odd day now and then, and I don't think I ever came to the gallery. My parents wanted to invite people back to the hotel after the funeral but everyone disappeared before they had the chance.'

'No one anticipated an invite so don't worry about that. Bill told us what he intended to do a long time ago. Have you come to take a closer look?'

'Yes, I suppose I have. I didn't know about his plans to leave it to me and

I'm also surprised to find the gallery is open.'

'We didn't know what to do, so Ben and I decided to carry on as usual until someone told us to do otherwise.'

'Ben?'

'Ben has worked here for longer than I have. He's our dogsbody. He does the repairs and paintwork, and he organizes deliveries and fetching new additions. He was standing next to me at the funeral.'

Kim nodded. 'I thought you were familiar, but I wasn't sure. I'm sorry, but I've forgotten your name.'

'Audrey, Audrey Westwood. I came whenever I was needed. In winter, Bill often just put up the 'closed' sign if he went out for a while, but in summer he needed a replacement more often. That's when we sold the most pictures.'

Kim nodded. It sounded like these two people had been helping Uncle Bill for a long time. She glanced around. 'Are these all the paintings?'

Audrey's laugh tinkled. 'Good heavens, no! There are dozens of canvases upstairs. Bill was too charitable for his own good. He bought paintings knowing there wasn't much of a chance of selling them. He knew most of the artists living in this area. Mind you, he was a good judge and was very knowledgeable. Sometimes he also bought pictures from house clearance sales. Most of them landed upstairs and were forgotten. Bill displayed what he thought tourists would buy, mostly local landscapes and seascapes.'

Being candid, Kim said, 'I haven't a clue about art or running a gallery.'

Audrey's eyes twinkled sympathetically. 'I know. A lot of people who own galleries these days don't, although they like to pretend they do.' She hesitated. 'Will you keep it?'

Kim shrugged. 'I don't know yet. Perhaps it would be sensible to let the money help charities. I came down to look around and think about it in peace.'

The older woman nodded. 'I understand. It's not easy for you to decide.

You're still young and this is a small seaside place. At this time of year, it probably won't be easy to find a buyer anyway. Where are you staying?'

'The Sailor's Arms, down by the harbour.'

'You could have saved your money. Bill always left a spare key here in case he locked himself out. I'm sure Don Wilson won't object to you staying in the cottage. It's yours until you decide otherwise. It's very picturesque, and Bill looked after it well. How long are you staying?'

'Until lunchtime tomorrow.'

'Well, I hope you'll find the right answer before you leave.'

Being her honest self, Kim answered, 'Knowing Uncle Bill employed other people doesn't make it any easier for me. If I sell, you and Ben will be out of a job.'

'Probably, but don't let that bother you. I was only here part-time anyway and Ben is a pensioner. He helped because he was Bill's friend. He'd miss it because he's a widower and it helped fill in his time, but he wouldn't lose much financially. Don't let that influence your decision. Do what's best for you. I'm sure Bill would have said the same if he was here.'

A passing couple stopped in front of the display window and came in. Audrey went towards them and stood quietly at a distance as they viewed the pictures. Now and then, they asked a question or commented on something. Finally, expressing their thanks, they left without buying anything.

Audrey came back and sighed softly. 'From a hundred people who come in for a closer look, one will buy something — if we're lucky. That's how it is in this business.' She straightened. 'Have a cup of tea and tell me about yourself.' Without waiting for a reply, she bustled off and Kim followed.

Audrey phoned Ben. By the time Audrey was pouring the tea into blue-and-white striped mugs, he had arrived. He was an elderly man with a craggy, lined face and deep-set blue eyes. He stooped slightly and took off his blue cotton sailor cap and hung it on a hook before he studied Kim for a moment. He held out his hand and in a gruff but not unfriendly tone he said, 'Bill talked a lot about you.'

She took his rough, tanned hand. 'Did he?'

'He watched you from afar. He was damned proud of you.'

Tears hovered when she thought about her godfather. She gulped some tea to steady herself. 'He was great. It was a shock for us when he died. Sixty-five is not old these days.'

Ben nodded. 'We didn't realize he had heart trouble. No one did. I'm glad he didn't suffer. I found him that morning when he didn't come to the gallery. I think that his main worry was that he'd go through some long and lingering illness before he died. I'm glad that didn't happen.'

'You were good friends?'

'Yes; Audrey and me, both of us.

Completely different backgrounds and characters of course, but we got on well. Your uncle was a cultivated gentleman.'

'I agree, and I can also see why Uncle Bill liked you. You can't buy loyalty and friendship; you have to earn them.'

Ben shuffled his feet. 'Have you decided whether or not to take it on?'

'Audrey and I were just talking about it. I'm here to decide.'

'To be honest, the gallery has never made much money. It's been even harder during the past couple of years because people have less money to spend on extras. But somehow Bill kept it going.' Ben took out a crumpled handkerchief and blew his nose. 'Audrey and I have talked about the situation, and whatever you decide is fine by us. You're very young and we realize you may not want to burden yourself with it. Neither of us depends on the gallery for our bread and butter. Audrey could have earned more filling the shelves at the local supermarket, and I helped out of friendship.'

Kim touched his arm briefly. 'Thanks!

That helps me to decide without a having a troubled conscience.'

Audrey held up the teapot. 'What about another cup?' Kim nodded and held out her mug for a refill. 'I'll give you the key and you can look around the cottage in your own time. The gallery is open from two until six on a Saturday and from two until five on Sundays. Don't worry if I'm not here when you leave. Pop the key through the letterbox; I'll find it on Monday. I live outside the village.'

Kim took a sip of tea and said, 'I just met someone called Mark Fraser in the churchyard.'

Ben chortled. 'Aha! The vultures are gathering!'

'You know him?'

'Mark grew up locally. He has a house just down the coast. One of the biggest houses around here.'

Audrey added, 'It's in a fabulous spot. Mark is okay. He sometimes gives strangers the impression that he's proud and arrogant, but he isn't.'

'He's in art?'

'Oh, yes. He has a posh place in Poole. He took over the family business after his father retired. We didn't think he'd come back; he was working in London at the time. But he did, and he's turned the place into a well-known focal point for modern art.'

Bill added, 'He deals with galleries in London and all over the world. He's clever — has made a name for himself and grown rich in the process. Bill always said he had his head screwed on the right way. He and Bill had differing aims. Bill wanted to sell pictures by local artists and encouraged new talent. Mark sees things internationally. He spends as much time away as he does at home.'

Audrey said, 'He wasn't so lucky personally. His ex-wife had an affair with an artist he represented. He's always been an upright character. He didn't forgive and forget. There was a forced separation and he instigated divorce proceedings, although apparently she tried

30

everything she could to get him back. It didn't work, and in the end she turned nasty and tried to squeeze every last penny out of him. Before it got to the final court proceedings, she drowned. There are lots of dangerous places with strong currents near here. No one was with her and they found her body on the rocks further down the coast. Mark was in New York at the time and had to come back to identify the body. She's buried near Reigate, where she came from.'

'So she wasn't a local?'

'No, they met in London. They were only married a year or two. No children. Her carryings-on upset him for a long time. Everyone sympathised, but you have to get through something like that on your own.'

'I suppose so.' Kim fingered her mug. 'He made me an offer for the gallery.'

Ben's eyebrows lifted. 'And?'

'I told him I hadn't decided. He warned me I wouldn't succeed. To be honest, he may be right.'

31

Ben grunted. 'Bill survived, didn't he? Most of his customers wanted to buy pictures they liked — something recognizable to hang on their walls. You can still get the paintings from the same people Bill used. If you want to be more adventurous, you can branch out and sell something different, once you feel more confident. Winter is always a quiet time of the year, so you'd have time to settle in. That's if you decide to stay, of course. I'm surprised Mark wants it. We're off the beaten track for his kind of customers, but he never does anything without a good reason. As to him predicting your downfall, it depends on how much you want to earn. If you want to get rich, forget it. If you want a fair income, you have a very good chance.'

Kim stayed a while. They chatted about her godfather and about the village. Ben explained that the village was a couple of hundred years old and inhabitants in early days supplemented their incomes by fishing and smuggling contraband from France.

She left them with the key in her pocket and knowing they'd talk about her when she left. She'd take a look inside Uncle Bill's cottage later. Apart from her parents, Ben was the first person who'd actually encouraged her. She didn't need an extravagant lifestyle. If she could make enough money to cover the overheads plus a bit extra for her needs, she'd be quite happy. The prospect of settling down in a quieter environment was tempting. Kim didn't want to admit it, but when she recalled Mark Fraser's words, it only wakened her fighting spirit. It'd be nice to make him sit up. Illogically, she suddenly decided that she wanted to take over, and she would.

3

Finishing her old life and moving to her new one went in a flash. After Kim gave notice at work and for her flat, every day and every week was full of extra jobs and formalities until she finally watched the small van drive away. She wondered if she was mad to leave her steady job for a life of the unknown. Her parents had come to help her clear the flat, and she was now ready to follow the van to Dulsworth.

'Are you sure you can manage?' her mother asked.

Kim gave her a hug. 'Of course, Mum. The removal men will carry the heavy things and I can unpack the boxes at my leisure. Thanks for storing the rest of the stuff in your garage until you can dispose of it. You've been wonderful. Come down and see me soon, whenever you like.'

'We will. Good luck!' She stroked her daughter's cheek. 'We are so glad you decided to take the gallery. Bill would have been delighted.'

Kim nodded. Her dad issued his usual instructions. 'Drive carefully! Let us know that you've arrived safely. We'll be home in less than an hour, our feet up with a cup of tea.'

'I will, promise!' She looked up at the blank windows of her former flat, kissed her parents' cheeks, and got into her car.

*   *   *

During the journey, Kim thought about the last couple of weeks. She'd given a farewell party in the office last Friday, and another for her closest friends last weekend. Some people were sceptical about her decision, while others were slightly envious.

Howard didn't question why she wanted her spare key back. He probably presumed it was because of her move.

She never bothered to talk about their relationship. She was leaving, and it was self-explanatory that they wouldn't be able to see each other anymore. He came to her party and promised to visit her soon. She hoped it was an empty promise. She was relieved to be on her way. There was no turning back now and there was also no point in worrying about whether it was the right decision.

She reached Dulsworth ahead of the removal van. It was early afternoon. The gallery was closed. She fingered the keys in her pocket. It was almost as if Uncle Bill was still alive. Walking up the crazy path, she finally opened the door. The cottage was fully furnished, with antique items that suited their background much better than anything she owned. She only intended to add her bed, a favourite easy chair, a dishwasher and the media centre.

There was a 'welcome' note from Audrey, a saucepan of soup on the stove, a loaf of bread on the table and some other essentials in the fridge. She was moved by the kindness of someone she hardly knew.

* * *

By Monday morning she'd emptied the packing cases and she went to the gallery. The weather wasn't encouraging, but she opened anyway. She took her laptop with her. As expected, it was quiet and no one called. She spread her papers over the table in the back room. She'd look for a suitable desk one day but, for the present, she'd share the space with the tea things.

Firstly, she needed to check Uncle Bill's records, contact his usual suppliers and talk to the bank manager. She decided to keep offering the kinds of pictures Uncle Bill favoured at present, but perhaps she'd branch out and sell other kinds later. It'd be terrific if she could discover a talented new artist. Perhaps she could even organize exhibitions. She chewed on the end of her pencil and made a few notes. She wanted to join the village community too. It would be lovely to find a niche in village life.

She'd read about art on the internet and tried to absorb some information so she wouldn't sound like a complete idiot. Art was so wide-ranging; she understood why dealers concentrated on one area. She also found that many gallery owners were artists or former artists. She looked out of the unadorned window onto the small back yard and decided her main aim was to develop a good reputation.

Audrey called in the afternoon for a chat. After Kim had thanked her profusely for the groceries and her welcome, Audrey asked, 'Any customers?'

Kim shook her head. 'No. Open all day, and not one.'

Audrey nodded. 'That's nothing unusual. At this time of year, business falls off. Don't let it get you down.'

She smiled. 'It won't. I can see Uncle Bill spread his income over the whole year, so we'll get through the winter quite comfortably, even if we don't sell another picture. Is there a list of the people who supplied the landscapes and seascapes, and information about the ones already hanging here? I looked in the cottage, but found nothing.'

'Over there in the cupboard in a green folder with names, addresses, telephone numbers, the prices he paid for various pictures, and their final selling prices. That might be a useful guide for you until you've found your feet. It's all there.'

'Wonderful. I'm going to visit some of them and introduce myself. Where's Ben? I haven't seen him since I arrived.'

'I'll tell him to call. I expect he wasn't certain if you still wanted him to come.'

'Of course I do. I need you both. I can't pay you much, but if you're willing to carry on as before, it'd be a great help.'

Audrey smiled broadly. 'Glad to help, my dear, and I'm sure Ben will be too.'

★　★　★

A few days later she'd already met most of the artists. They were a friendly, co-operative bunch. Most of them had regular jobs and only painted in their spare time because they couldn't exist from painting full-time.

★　★　★

Returning one day from a visit, Kim re-opened the gallery and put the kettle on to boil. About to pour the water into the teapot, she heard the bell tinkle and heavy footsteps. Perhaps this time it was someone who'd actually come to buy something. She went to look. Her hopes died a quick death, and colour mounted her cheeks when she recognized Mark Fraser.

The top of his head nearly touched the ceiling and his soft overcoat flowed around his tall, athletic physique as he walked towards her. He had a large potted green plant decorated with an extravagant red bow.

'Morning! I wanted to wish you

luck!' He held the plant towards her and she was too surprised to do anything but accept it.

'Thank you.' She paused for a second. 'I must admit I'm surprised to see you. I thought you'd never speak to me again, after I refused your offer.'

He smiled, and the withdrawn and reserved expression vanished. She liked the result and the difference it made to his looks.

'No one can afford to hold grudges. We're bound to meet now and then. Did you expect that I'd ignore you, or even set out to wreck your chances?' His eyes twinkled. 'I could tell you were determined the day we met so I'm not surprised you decided to take it on. We don't cover the same area so I'm definitely no competition.'

She was glad. He was probably a very hard-hitting businessman. 'Would you like a cup of tea? I'm just making some.' As far as she knew, he hadn't scuttled her beginnings and it didn't sound like he intended to either.

He looked at his watch. 'Yes, I would.'

She deposited the plant on the floor near the window. 'Follow me!'

He did, and glanced at the pictures on display. Over her shoulder he remarked, 'You haven't changed much yet. Do you intend to stick to Bill's ideas, or break out?'

She gestured to an old-fashioned kitchen chair and he sat down. 'I'm still trying to decide what I want to do. I haven't planned any momentous changes yet. Milk? Sugar?'

He nodded. 'Yes, please — both; one spoonful of sugar. If you want an opinion or advice, just ask.'

She picked up her cup. His good looks and confident manner attracted her, but she was on her guard about the rest. 'I'm grateful for your offer, but puzzled why you should want to help. In a way we're rivals, aren't we?'

He laughed softly. 'I'm not interested in the kind of customers who buy your sort of pictures.'

'That's very patronizing. Not everyone can afford astronomical prices for an item of conceptual or abstract art that they don't understand.'

'Aha! You've been studying the market.'

'Just some of the terminology. I admit I don't even understand the differences yet, especially about modern art.'

He leaned forward and said softly, 'Know something? Neither do I. Trends and terminology change overnight. It's hard to keep up with it all sometimes.' He looked at her for a second. 'You're very direct, aren't you? Not many people who hardly know me would have enough gumption to call me patronizing.'

'Blame that on my forefathers. They came from the north, where people call a spade a spade. People tell me I never beat about the bush.'

He ran his hand over his jaw-line. 'Ordinary people buy what they like, what they can afford and what they understand, and that's fine by me, even though you might not think so. I mostly deal with people who know nothing about what they're buying, and ask few questions apart from the price and if the person who created it is famous.'

'That's sad, isn't it? Imagine buying pictures to hang on your wall that you care nothing about.' She studied his face. She wanted to keep her distance. She couldn't figure out why he was wasting his time with her. He attracted her, and that wasn't merely because he looked good. She felt annoyed with herself. She dragged her glance from his face and concentrated on what he was saying.

'That's how it is in this business, especially among people who invest in art. Usually they're individuals, or even companies, with too much money and the need to bunker their riches in property, jewellery or art. Andy Warhol once said, 'good business is the best art.''

Kim laughed. 'That sounds unscrupulous.'

'Perhaps, but a lot of rich artists become famous through art galleries. They've always been platforms. That's where dealers come in; it's the exciting part. I'm still hoping that one day I'll find another Warhol, Lichtenstein, Macke, Delaunay or someone similar.'

'What about someone like van Gogh? He didn't have much luck. He only ever sold one painting in his lifetime, didn't he?'

Tipping his head to the side, Mark replied, 'Perhaps he wasn't lucky enough to find the right person to sell his stuff.'

She laughed. 'I hear you have a gallery in Poole.'

His jaw tensed. He hugged the cup tighter with his long fingers. 'I see that the grapevine has been busy. Yes, I took it over from my father when he retired.'

She wished she hadn't mentioned it. He was probably very touchy about his personal life. He also lived with the knowledge that people gossiped about him and his ex-wife.

The musical tones of his mobile

interrupted any further conversation. He replied brusquely, 'Okay, I'm on my way. I'll be there in about an hour.' He closed his phone with a snap and stood up. 'Sorry! That was Gloria, my assistant. Business calls again. Thanks for the tea.'

'You're welcome, and thanks for the plant. It was a very kind thought.'

A glint of humour returned to his expression. 'A pleasure! I hope you'll call at my gallery one day. I'll be pleased to show you around.'

She couldn't imagine going out of her way to do that. They lived in different worlds. It wasn't likely that they'd meet socially very often. He was well-off, and money was no object among the kind of people he knew. She followed him to the door and waited until he got into his car. She saw him lift his hand before he drove off quickly down the alleyway. She mused that he knew his way around the little town better than she did.

4

Business was slack. Kim almost did a somersault when she sold a picture several days later. By now she'd almost worked her way through the list of Uncle Bill's suppliers. She'd either phoned or visited them.

One afternoon, after sitting around being bored, she decided to check the paintings upstairs. Perhaps she could use some of them to fill gaps on the wall if she ran out of other pictures. It might also help to widen the choice on offer.

She looked from the top of the stairs. Everything was covered in a thick layer of dust and she decided to postpone cleaning until Monday when visitors were unlikely. She gazed down the cobwebbed corridor. If she didn't make enough money, she could turn the upstairs into a holiday flat. There were three rooms. It would mean investing some of her savings to install an open kitchen in one room, and refurbish the bathroom, but Dulsworth was a popular holiday resort, and accommodation was restricted. The entrance door faced the stairs, and she'd need to make some kind of separate entrance, but it was a real possibility.

She checked her watch and decided to close the gallery and visit one of the last names on Uncle Bill's list.

★　★　★

Kim had difficulty finding him because he lived in a fisherman's cottage off the beaten track. The view of the coast from his untidy garden was breathtaking. The rough cliffs fell in vertical swoops down into tiny sanded bays. The weather was good and the sea was a kaleidoscope of blues and greens. She knocked on the weather-beaten door several times before it opened. He was young with a friendly, bantering expression.

'Morning! Adrian Calderwood?'

'Yes, what can I do for you?'

She noticed some spots of paint on his check shirt. She explained who she was.

'I heard that Bill had died. He was a fine person. I didn't find out until it was too late to come to the funeral. You run the gallery now?'

'Yes, I'm making the rounds of the people he listed. I'm afraid I've never seen any of your paintings. Uncle Bill must have sold them.'

He laughed and his eyes twinkled. 'I doubt it. I think he bought the ones he did out of kindness. Perhaps he threw them away when he got home.'

'You're a full-time artist?' She enjoyed his relaxed manner.

'Sort of. I teach evening classes and I organize resident summer courses at a local hotel. The money keeps my head above water for the rest of the year. Would you like a cup of coffee?'

'If you're sure I'm not disturbing you.'

'I'm doing what I'm always doing — I'm painting, but I need a break. If you go around the corner, there's a sunny bench hidden from the wind.'

He disappeared and she found the sunny corner. He was right; it was a delightful spot. He returned with two mugs of instant coffee. She took one.

'Thanks! You are one of the few artists I've met who paints full-time.'

'I studied art in London and expected to take the world by storm. I soon found out I was daydreaming. I carry on painting because I can't stop! I don't dwell on the fact that I'm one of thousands, all dreaming of recognition.'

'What kind of art do you focus on?'

'I enjoy experimenting. At the moment I'm dabbling in abstract art, but I don't feel very comfortable with it. I usually follow my flights of imagination. I'll show you some canvasses before you leave, if you like.'

'I know nothing about art, so don't expect me to shower you with praise.'

He burst out laughing. 'You run an art gallery and don't want to give me an opinion?'

'I know what I like and I'm interested.'

He stuck his leg out in a straight line and studied her carefully in silence. 'I've always been fascinated by beautiful women. I'd like to paint you. A real portrait. I haven't done one for a while.'

'I'm not beautiful.' She hoped he wasn't flattering her just because he hoped she'd continue to buy his paintings.

'Perhaps beautiful is going too far, but you're extremely attractive and your chestnut hair and grey eyes are definitely beautiful. It's not just physical aspects that make a person beautiful; it's their inner qualities.'

She felt uncomfortable with his directness, but realized that in his milieu it was nothing unusual. She gestured towards the coast and the cliffs. 'You have wonderful things to paint. What a place to live.'

He looked towards the wild coastline. 'Yes, it's great, isn't it? The cottage used to belong to my great uncle. No one else wanted it when he died.

No one else wanted to buy it either, because it needs a complete overhaul. In the end, the family didn't object to me moving in, otherwise it would have fallen into complete disrepair. If I ever have enough money, I'll get an estimate and buy the others out. It's a godsend for me because I can't afford to live anywhere else, and the isolation is perfect for painting. It's punishing here in the winter, but if you don't mind storms, cold winds, and leaky window frames, it's wonderful. I've painted the cliffs more times than I care to remember.'

She smiled. 'I'd like to see some of your paintings before I leave, if I'm not interrupting.'

'Of course not. I'm always prepared to show off a bit!'

'If you don't blow your own trumpet, no one else will.'

He smiled and she got up to follow him indoors. He said, 'I hope you'll visit me again, even if you don't like my paintings. I don't get many visitors.'

'I can't promise to come, or buy your

pictures, but I'll try!'

'Come and look.' He threw his remaining coffee in an arc into a nearby bush and preceded her into the cottage.

Kim needed a moment to adjust to the darkness, but Adrian went ahead through the one main room into to a kind of lean-to glasshouse. Canvasses were stacked in rows, and painting utensils of all kinds were piled on an old-fashioned kitchen table in the middle. The easel held a picture full of blatant colours in a jumble of squares, triangles, and oblongs.

She considered it for a moment. 'I won't pretend I understand what you're trying to say, but I love the colours and the arrangement.'

He walked to a line of canvases and pulled one out at random. This time Kim could recognize various items that had been painted on top of and into each other in a fluid movement. Adrian stood it against the wall and pulled out another one. It was the head and shoulders of an old woman with a scarf tied round her head. The colours were sombre and the lines were not precise, but the woman's facial expression was wonderful. Anyone could tell life had not always been kind to her. Kim was impressed

'Gosh! What a range.'

He grinned. 'I can even paint flowers. I have to. Most of the students on my courses are women, and they tell me what they want to paint. Mostly I give in, and sacrifice my idea of getting them to paint what they feel, not what they see.'

An idea began to materialize in Kim's mind. 'Have you ever thought about having a one-man exhibition?'

'I've contributed towards local exhibitions, but I couldn't finance one of my own. I'd have to hire a suitable place, advertise, provide refreshments, and so on.'

Kim was thoughtful. 'I must say, I like your work. It's different.'

'I'm glad you like it. Come again, whenever you like. We can go out for a drink together one evening, if you pay.'

She laughed. 'Perhaps!' She considered him for a moment. 'I always imagined artists were bohemian beings — disorderly, unkempt and reckless.'

'You've seen too many old movies.' He pinched the material of his shirt. 'I mess myself up, but I am organized. I can't afford to be reckless or eccentric.' He paused for a moment. 'By the way, if you're looking for other kinds of art, visit Brian Solway and his wife Melanie. They're friends of mine. He's a sculptor and Melanie's a potter. They live in Ilsworth. They make interesting stuff. I know Bill only sold paintings, but you could offer other kinds of art as well.'

Kim was surprised when he kissed her cheek before she left. He noticed and tilted his head to the side with a knowing smile. He smelt of soap and linseed oil. She liked him. He was uncomplicated, charming and nice. She had a lot to think about.

⋆   ⋆   ⋆

Monday was grey and overcast. There was little chance of visitors. Kim hauled her cleaner up the stairs. There were three rooms and a small old-fashioned bathroom. The bath was stained and the toilet and wash basin were in a terrible state. The two main rooms were separated by an arched doorway. The hum of the cleaner filled the air as Kim removed the dust and cobwebs. As soon as she could move around without sending up clouds of dust, she fetched a bucket of soapy water, some dusters, and a notebook and pencil. She cleaned the rooms and began to examine the paintings. Some were dreadful, but others were okay. If she could decipher a signature, she made a note of it. She restacked them into two piles: ones she liked, and ones she didn't. They were nearly all oil paintings.

She wondered why Uncle Bill had never displayed them. Perhaps he'd even forgotten they were here. Gradually she worked her way through the first room and moved into the second, cleaning and dusting as she went.

She was delighted when she found a couple of Adrian Calderwood's pictures. She looked at them carefully. There were two scenes of the cliffs, a still-life of some glasses, and one portrait of an elderly man with a weathered skin and blue eyes. She didn't know how good they were, but an idea began to form in her head. She'd hold an exhibition of his paintings, and perhaps she'd add some sculpture and pottery by the people he mentioned.

She sat back on her heels and began to think about what was involved. She couldn't hold a permanent exhibition, but a one-man show for a couple of days was a possibility. There wasn't much happening at this time of year anyway. She'd advertise it using self-made posters and try to involve the local newspaper, the local radio, and the library. Adrian would help her hang the pictures. They were unframed, but that didn't lessen their appeal. She'd need some small pedestals if she displayed small pieces of sculpture or items of pottery. Ben would make those. She felt a surge of excitement. A small advert in a specialist art magazine might not be too expensive and could attract someone important.

She'd offer coffee, cider and mineral water. No one who came to review an unknown artist in an obscure gallery would expect exclusive refreshments.

When she finished, she moved the pile of paintings she liked over to the cottage and put the rest together in one room. She now had an extra room to display some of Adrian's paintings. Ben and Audrey would help. She wondered what they'd think about her idea. The walls needed redecorating. Plain white walls would be perfect. Her dad was a whiz at papering.

The idea was exciting. She'd visit Adrian tomorrow and see what he thought, and stop off to visit the sculptor and his wife on the way back.

5

Kim felt elated.

She hadn't expected the evening to be such a success. The place was packed. Conversation hummed and there was a lively atmosphere. Audrey was in charge of serving the drinks and Ben of replenishing them. There were big bowls of crisps and biscuits positioned throughout the gallery for people to help themselves.

Adrian seemed delighted and was busy talking to various people about his paintings. After a while, he came across and threw an arm round Kim's shoulder.

'I can't thank you enough. It's amazing. When you suggested a one-man show, I wondered if it'd be worth it, but you've attracted exactly the right kind of people.'

She laughed softly. 'I'm pleased too.

It's my first show! Everyone I've talked to loves your pictures. But it wouldn't have happened without you! I've already sold two paintings, and the evening's just begun. Someone I just talked to wants to buy your picture of the cliffs at sunset hanging upstairs.'

'Really? Smashing! By the look of things, you could have asked for more money for them, but you'll have to stick to your price list now.'

She nodded. 'I'm happy to sell anything at the moment.'

'I'm not greedy. You must let me pay for the drinks. I couldn't afford it before, but I can now.' He gave her a wide smile and kissed her cheek.

'Evening!' A deep voice interrupted them. Kim was flustered to see Mark Fraser.

'Hello, Mark. Nice to see you. This is Adrian Calderwood, the star of the show. I expect you know each other, both of you being local residents.'

Mark held out his hand. 'Hi! I've seen your summer courses advertised but I've never seen any of your paintings before. I've just had a quick look around. Impressive!'

Adrian looked pleased. 'I've heard of your gallery of course.' He tightened his grip around Kim's shoulders. 'If it hadn't been for this young lady, this wouldn't have happened. She's wonderful.'

Mark looked around quickly. 'Yes, it looks like she's done everything right. That chap over there is from a well-known gallery in Manchester. He probably saw a poster somewhere. That's how I found out about it too.'

'Really?' Kim and Adrian followed the direction of his eyes. The man was examining one of the paintings closely.

Kim said, 'I put a small advert in a specialist magazine; perhaps he saw that.'

Mark's eyebrows lifted. 'Good for you. Take my advice, though — if he starts haggling, take no notice. He's a bit of a fox and he knows exactly when something is good. Don't let him bargain.

Tell him you're thinking of putting a reserve on the painting. I bet he'll give in and pay up.'

'Wow!' Adrian exclaimed. 'Years of evening classes and summer courses, and now one evening like this!'

Audrey sidled up to them. 'Kim, we're running out of cider.'

'I've plenty over in the cottage. When I explained to the supplier what it was for, he left a stack of boxes. He said he'd sort out the bill when he comes to pick up the remains. Will you ask Ben to help me fetch it, please?'

Mark seemed amused. 'That's a nice touch. A local drink. Need any help?'

She shook her head. 'No, it's only next door and I think I'm still capable of carrying a box of bottles.'

With traces of dry amusement in his voice, Mark turned to Adrian. 'How about showing me the pictures I haven't seen yet? The ones upstairs?'

'With pleasure. Follow me.'

6

Mark stood and held Kim's glance. His voice was smooth but insistent. 'I thought it'd be fair to tell you before I talk to Adrian. You were the one who found him.'

She stared, wide-eyed. Her throat was dry. She was happy for Adrian and hoped she didn't sound mean. Feeling tight-lipped, she replied, 'I'm glad. I know I can't provide him with enough support. I also understand why you want to represent him. I think his work is good, and I'm proud I gave him his first real chance via this gallery.' Her colour heightened. 'If I'd been in business longer I might have fought you for the right. I won't. I wish him lots of success. I'd never stand in his way.' She turned and pretended to straighten one of the paintings.

He stood with his hands in his pockets. 'I realize that it sounds like I've pinched him, but . . . ' He hesitated for a moment.

Kim turned back towards him abruptly and took an unsteady breath. It was silly to act immaturely. Unconsciously, she moved back a step. 'Please don't sympathize. It all comes down to business in the end, doesn't it? I wish him well.'

His mouth tightened a fraction. 'A while back, you told me that you had no immediate ambitions beyond selling local art. I didn't think you'd mind if I took him on. He has bags of talent and he deserves a wider, more appreciative audience. I've a feeling he might have a great career ahead of him. Nothing will change the fact that you helped make that possible. I'm sure he'll always remember that.'

The burst of antagonism faded. He was right. She couldn't give Adrian the support he needed. Her irritation was generated because Mark had snapped him up. It made her wonder if he'd been friendly with intent. Perhaps he always used connections and friendship to feather his own nest. First and foremost, Mark Fraser was probably a businessman who grabbed each opportunity as it came along.

Aware that he needed to smooth the atmosphere, he asked, 'How many paintings did he sell?'

'Six of his own and two of the ones Uncle Bill bought from him years ago.'

'Well, hang on to any others you may have. They might be worth a lot more in a couple of years' time.'

'Are you on your way to see Adrian now?'

'I was, but I phoned him and found he's out, so I'll contact him later.'

'Good! Say hello from me when you do.'

He looked around. 'How's business?'

She didn't understand why he was interested, but she guessed he was automatically curious about any business in the same sphere as his own. He wasn't a man who used a lot of pointless chit-chat.

'Like it always is in the week at this time of the year. I may see a customer browsing around nearer the weekend — if I'm lucky.'

Friendly, smiling, and bantering in a relaxed manner, he said, 'Then put up the 'closed' sign and get your coat. I'll take you out for a Devonshire tea.'

She felt breathless for a moment and then decided that it'd be silly to refuse him. He most likely wanted to compensate. Despite her reservations about him, for some reason she liked the idea of spending time with him. 'That is always a treat.'

'Then hurry up!'

★　★　★

The car smelt of leather and Mark's aftershave. He looked across and gave Kim a smile. Her insides took a dive and she warned herself not to get involved. He was not her type at all, and his wife had probably damaged his attitude to women forevermore. She certainly didn't intend to pay him extra attention, but accepting his invitation already meant that her body wasn't really listening to her head.

The car ate up the miles. They finally stopped at a small tearoom. It was empty. Mark chose a table near a small window looking out to sea. The middle-aged owner bustled out as soon as they arrived.

'Two teas, please,' Mark told her. 'And all the trimmings.'

The handful of tables had crisp blue-and-white tablecloths and a single pink carnation in the middle. Kim remarked, 'This is nice.'

'Yes, I come here often. Alone, or sometimes with a customer if I want to impress them. Their scones are unbeatable.'

She asked jestingly, 'Is that why you brought me here? To impress me?'

His expression quietened. 'I don't think anyone would impress you with a plateful of scones and a dollop of cream, would they?'

Her eyes sparkled and she shook her head.

'This tearoom tops my list at present,' he said. His smile softened his features and when his eyes met hers, they were cheerful.

She relaxed. 'In other words, you're a cream tea junkie?'

He gave a throaty laugh and specks of darker colour twinkled in the depths of his eyes. 'Probably! It certainly looks like it, doesn't it? I try not to indulge too often, though, otherwise I'd end up looking like the back end of a bus!'

Kim considered his tall, athletic physique and thought that would be a great pity. She pushed a wayward strand of auburn hair off her forehead. 'I gather you travel a lot. Do you mind?'

He shrugged. 'It depends where I have to go, and why. Gloria does a lot of the travelling these days. She says she enjoys it. As long as we're on the same wavelength business-wise, that's fine with me. The range and number of customers has increased since I took over from my father. A lot more people come to me these days. Sometimes a computer conference saves a journey, and sending example pictures via emails cuts out a lot of the initial haggling too.'

'I don't suppose you can just turn the sign on the door and take off, like I do.'

'True! We're training a part-time student to cover for us if we're away at the same time. He's shaping up very well. I still cover most of the long-distance hauls, but I don't mind. There's nothing holding me back.' He paused and to her surprise, he said, 'You know about my ex-wife?'

Kim felt flustered and admired his candour. 'Yes. I'm sorry. It was probably a very difficult time for you. I heard you were in the process of divorce proceedings and she drowned.'

He looked out of the window briefly. 'Yes, that's about right.'

'Does anyone know what actually happened?'

'Romantics like to believe she got

careless because she was in the depths of amorous despair.'

'And you?' She didn't know how far she could query, but he'd started the conversation and he was capable of ending it if he wanted to.

He shrugged. 'Who knows? Our marriage had collapsed. She was a good swimmer and she knew about the dangerous currents. No one will ever know the truth.' He sounded detached and impersonal.

'What was she like?'

'Beautiful, wilful, and pig-headed. She loved the social aspect of my work, but had no interest in how I earned the money. She didn't work, got bored easily, and had no interests to keep her occupied. She looked for amusement elsewhere. She worked in London as a model until we married. She was used to never-ending parties and social gatherings. She found life around here very tedious. I didn't reckon with that.' He looked tight-lipped and grim. Evidently, the memories weren't pleasant ones. He straightened and asked,

'What about you? Have you got a serious boyfriend?'

She shook her head. 'Not at the moment. It's not easy to meet someone who's completely on your wavelength, is it? These days people can't imagine loving the same person for longer than weeks or months. I'm just too choosy.'

The warmth of his smile echoed in his voice. 'I'm sure you'll meet someone who'll knock you off your feet one day.'

'Well, I don't think I've increased my chances by moving to Dulsworth. The population seems to be another generation.'

Mark burst out laughing. 'That's not true.'

The owner interrupted to spread the tea things on the table. The scones were still steaming; they'd just come out of the oven.

Kim commented, 'Mmm, this looks good.'

'There are just as many young people living in the village as in any other place,' Mark continued. 'The young men from

Dulsworth will soon be invading your gallery pretending to be interested in the paintings, but actually hoping to ask you out.' He pointed towards her plate and seemed contented in her company. 'The Devonshire method is to split the scone, cover each half with cream and then the jam. Have you ever heard of thunder-and-lightning?'

'No, what's that?' She was already busy with her knife.

He watched with interest as she took her first bite. 'What do you think?'

'Mm, it's scrumptious!' She cleared a spot of jam from the corner of her mouth and Mark smiled.

'Thunder-and-lightening is a round of bread topped with clotted cream and golden syrup, honey or treacle.'

'Sounds fantastic, but it'll be difficult to top this.'

'I know a place not far from here where they make delicious thunder-and-lightning with home-made bread and natural honey. Another time perhaps?'

The prospect of spending another

afternoon like this with Mark was very appealing. 'Yes. That would be fun, I'm sure. Honey dripping down my chin in wide rivulets!'

Mark smiled and began to attack his own tea. He asked about Kim's family and mentioned he had an older sister living in South Africa. His parents had retired and moved to Bournemouth.

Waiting until her mouth was empty, Kim asked, 'Did you know much about art before you took over your father's business?'

'A little. I studied history and the history of art, but I didn't know what to do with my degree when I had it. I started to take more interest in the gallery and found I enjoyed that very much. It's still the case today.' He put down his knife and looked at his oblong Swiss watch. 'Tell you what, how about viewing my place after tea? There's not much point in you re-opening your shop today. I live near the village, so I'll drive you home afterwards.'

She was tempted. Much to her

surprise, she began to genuinely like him. There was a nice person hidden behind his serious expression. 'Haven't you anything better to do?'

He tilted his head to the side and grinned. 'No, not really! Not today.'

'All right. Why not?' Now that she felt more comfortable with him, she asked what she always wanted to know. 'Why did you want Bill's gallery? You don't need it. You already have a going concern in Poole.'

He answered without hesitation, 'In the first place, because I didn't want to see another gallery closing down. Secondly, when I pull out of the Poole gallery one day, I'd like somewhere like Bill's, not too far away, to keep me occupied. I'd display the kind of art I like.'

'So you would have kept it going?'

He spread some jam carefully on his scone and looked up to meet her glance straight on. 'Yes. I would have changed the concept and employed someone else until I could handle things myself. I would have displayed pictures that might not be to your taste. I intended to display realistic art alongside more progressive stuff. I'm glad to see you intend to widen the style of pictures on offer, even if you probably won't go as far as I would have done.'

She hoped her smile was noncommittal. 'I don't intend to include any modern art at present, because I don't understand it.'

He laughed softly. 'Neither did I in the beginning. Perhaps that'll change in time.'

They finished their cream tea at their leisure.

7

The powerful engine swallowed up the miles. Even though the roads were narrow, Mark was completely in control. He obviously knew the area very well. He knew when to slow down and when to accelerate without risk. They reached the outskirts of Poole and he pointed out various places of interest.

It was late afternoon. Shadows were lengthening as they walked the last meters to his gallery. The soft material of his coat brushed Kim now and again. It gave her an intimate feeling that was unexplainable, and silly!

* ★ ★

The shop wasn't far from the natural harbour, and his gallery was impressive. There was one solitary modern painting displayed in the window. It was an eye-catcher. The colours were beautiful and the shapes and forms were clear-cut and interesting.

Mark opened the door and stood aside for her to enter. The room was a mini-malistic display area with down-lights, white walls and plenty of space between the handful of modern paintings and sculptures on view. One piece of pottery in particular caught Kim's eye. Mark noticed her interest and explained.

'That's a purse vase by Anita Harris. The design is over ten years old. It's Poole pottery. Nice, isn't it? Someone asked us to sell it and it makes a pleasing focal point among all the paintings.'

'Yes. It's a lovely colour and the glaze is beautiful.' She looked around. A wide staircase led to an upper gallery. In one corner was a small office area with business files arranged along the rear wall. A handful of paintings filled the remaining space. 'Very elegant. Less is more?'

He laughed softly. 'Yes, I suppose that's a fitting description. We never display many canvasses at any one time. Our prices only attract a certain type of customer, and they know where to find us. Occasional visitors from the street are very rare.'

'That's not surprising, is it? When people see one painting on display, they rightly assume the gallery is too exclusive for day-trippers.'

'Perhaps. We aim to sell to a rich clientele and the appearance probably does stop casual visitors. It's a pity, but you can't have it both ways — an exclusive gallery that also caters to the masses.'

Someone sauntered down the stairs on high heels. She was slim, blond and wore a black shift dress, a gold necklace and matching thick bracelet. Each stride of her long legs was fluid and accentuated.

'Ah! Gloria, this is Kim Spenser. She took over a gallery in Dulsworth recently. I told you about her the other day.'

The woman glanced at him before

she held out her hand to Kim. Kim held the perfectly manicured, red-tipped hand for a moment. 'Hi! Nice to meet you.'

Gloria's answering smile didn't reach her eyes. Clearly, she was irritated that Mark had brought a strange woman to the gallery. How did she cope when he dealt with female customers who expected to be indulged or flattered?

Kim said, 'The gallery is lovely. Very Spartan, and extremely attractive. A visitor automatically concentrates on the items on offer.'

Gloria nodded but didn't comment. She turned to Mark. Her facial expression was suddenly lively. 'Lowoods rang just now. They've decided to take that pair of ink drawings. They tried to push the price down again but I told them there was no chance of you agreeing.'

He snapped his fingers. 'Good! I thought so. They made too many enquiries to be indifferent. They've probably got a collector lined up. I'm going up to London tomorrow. Have you got time to pack them for me before you leave tonight?

I'll take them with me and save the transport and insurance costs.' He turned to Kim. 'Gloria is the backbone of this place. I can't imagine what I'd do without her.'

Gloria gave a wooden laugh and touched his arm briefly. 'You know that flattery works every time, don't you? I'll organize it straight away.'

Kim turned away from them and wandered down the room and up the stairs. They might want to discuss something she shouldn't hear, so she gave them the chance.

★ ★ ★

Mark dropped Kim off outside her cottage. She thought briefly about inviting him in for supper, but didn't. They'd been together most of the day already. He might think she was pushing for his attention, and she wasn't. He was going to London tomorrow so he'd most likely make an early start.

He solved her uncertainty by saying,

'I think I'll drive straight on and try to see Adrian this evening. I'm busy the rest of the week.'

She picked up her shoulder bag and turned towards him. 'Thank you for that delicious tea, and the guided tour of your gallery.'

'A pleasure.' He started to get out.

She stopped him by touching his arm briefly. 'Please, don't. I'm fine. Oh — will you please tell Adrian he'll have to wait to take his photos? My sister is making a blitz visit this weekend, so I haven't any time.'

'Photos?'

She grinned. 'He has this mad idea about painting my portrait, and he told me he always takes lots of pictures to capture the fundamentals. He says he doesn't need dozens of sittings. Apparently, photos are a great help. I can't imagine why he wants to paint me in the first place.'

Mark's gaze travelled over her face. 'I do.'

She felt flustered. Her heart jolted.

'I'll probably end up as a blue blob on a green background.' He was so close to her that she felt the heat from his body.

He said softly, 'No I don't think so. I've seen a couple of his portraits and they're very good. I'm taking some of his stuff with me tomorrow to show a friend of mine. I hope it'll stir some interest. I'll give him your message.'

'Thanks.' She opened the door. 'Have a successful trip.'

He nodded. 'I'll be in touch.'

She got out in a hurry, almost glad to escape the invisible web of attraction he was spinning. He wasn't the kind of man she ought to like. He was too complex and she was too down-to-earth.

He drove off and she waited until the car's tail-lights disappeared. She was getting increasingly confused about him. He was a hard-headed businessman with a complicated past, but there was something about him she couldn't ignore and couldn't reject. She wondered what he thought about her. Sitting opposite her in the teashop this afternoon, Mark Fraser was a completely different person from what she had expected. He wasn't just jagged edges and complicated aloofness.

8

Trade didn't improve, although they sold two aquarelles and one painting during the following two weeks.

Kim began to hang some of the paintings from upstairs between the usual things on offer and also used the upstairs room as an additional display area. Gradually it paid off. People stayed longer because there was more variety. The seascapes and landscapes had the kind of conformity and pale colours that encouraged the observer to fly across them and look at the darker oil paintings. The darker oil paintings egged people on to study the wispy aquarelles more closely.

Uncle Bill had bought the oil paintings many years ago, so she had to guess today's selling price.

★　★　★

One day, Adrian called to take her photo. 'Mark's visit to London hasn't led to anything yet. One of the galleries he deals with did agree to display one or two paintings for a couple of weeks.'

'That's a good sign, isn't it? It's difficult to get a foot in the door in London.'

Adrian nodded. 'I'm keeping my fingers crossed that something definite develops. Mark warned me not to expect too much. He's right, but I can't help hoping.'

She smiled. 'Don't be impatient. Think how long some artists waited until they were recognized. Some never were.'

He focussed the camera and took some more snapshots. She felt very self-conscious. 'You don't have to paint me, Adrian. I honestly think you could find a more rewarding subject.'

'Shut up and keep still! I want to. Keeping busy is the best way to stop me thinking about London all the time.' She laughed.

He looked outside. 'Let's go down to the harbour. The light is still good. Outdoor photos are always better.'

She looked at her watch. 'Hey, I'm supposed to be running a business!'

'Not in the lunch hour. Put up the 'closed' sign. I'll treat you to a drink down the pub.'

She smiled. 'Okay.' She enjoyed Adrian's company and there wasn't much chance of a visitor so close to lunchtime. Perhaps she wouldn't be able to take spontaneous breaks later on, during the holiday season.

After Kim treated Adrian to a pub lunch, he left and she came back to the gallery. She settled down with her computer to search for some of the names she'd noted on the paintings from the upstairs rooms. It was time-consuming and she was pleased when she found any information. She copied the details to display with the picture. Daylight was fading fast when she closed her laptop for the day and shut the gallery.

* * *

Some people in the village were beginning to recognize her. She'd even been to church last week, something she hadn't done for ages. She decided to join the local historical society that evening and had already joined the library.

She made a quick, filling meal of pasta and then set out for the village hall, where the historical society met monthly. People looked up in surprise when she entered, but they welcomed her warmly. They put her firmly in their midst and she listened to their latest challenge. They were looking into the history of a disused mine in the neighbourhood. They were mostly older people. Tom and Ella were roughly her own age. She went with them to the pub for a farewell drink when the meeting broke up and Ella asked if she'd like to come for a walk along the coastal path on Sunday afternoon. Kim nodded and felt happy. Ignoring everyone and staying at home every night would get her nowhere.

*　　*　　*

Sunday afternoon Audrey came to the gallery for a few hours. Kim set off to meet Ella at the appointed spot. She was a teacher in the local primary school and good company. The cloudy sky cleared a little, and most of the time they wandered side by side. The route was well trodden and Kim enjoyed being out in the fresh air. She glanced continually towards the grey sea as they went along. Soon the two women knew a lot about each other. They rounded a headland and Kim spotted a large sprawling house a little way off the cliff. It had soft grey stone walls and rows of diamond-paned windows. There was grass and a low hedge dividing it from the public pathway, but Kim was certain the views from the house would be impressive.

Golden chrysanthemums filled some large terracotta pots standing in sheltered corners, and some hardy evergreen plants and heathers defied the onslaught of the sea winds along the edge of the terrace. Someone had managed, by knowledge or luck, to plant and sustain the right kind of plants and trees. Three stone steps led down from the wide stone terrace to the lawn. Its surround was a riot of heathers blooming in a variety of autumn colours.

The path suddenly dipped out of sight. Kim noticed the estuary down below. The rocks were all angles and jagged lines. The tide was on the turn and the water was beginning to flow up the mouth of the river. She looked at the house again and commented, 'What a lovely place! It looks ancient.'

Ella followed her glance. 'Yes, at least three hundred years old, probably a lot older. It stayed in the same family all that time. The last one died about five years ago; that's when Mark bought it.'

'Mark?'

'Mark Fraser. Have you met him? He's an art dealer in Poole.'

'Yes, I have.'

'Mark's nice. He crept into a shell for

a while after his wife died, but that was understandable. He's very likeable when you know him.'

Kim nodded and looked more carefully at the mullioned windows.

Ella looked ahead. 'The tide is turning fast. What shall we do? We can either turn back, or cross the rocks as fast as we can and walk back via the road.'

They were interrupted when Mark came out onto the terrace with a mug in his hand. He was wearing jeans and a faded blue work shirt. Kim liked the casual look on him. His brows lifted when he looked across in their direction. He then came down the steps and up to the hedge.

'Hi, Ella! How are things?' He nodded at Kim. 'Hi!'

Ella smiled at him. 'We're out for a walk.'

'So I see. I didn't realize you two knew each other.'

'We didn't until this week,' Ella told him. 'Kim joined the historical society and I suggested a hike along the coastal path today.'

'Oh, I see.' He looked towards the estuary. 'Well, you can't go much further now without getting your feet wet. The tide's coming in.'

'Yes, we were just wondering whether to cross the rocks and go back along the main road, or turn back.'

'What about a short rest and a mug of coffee instead?'

Ella smiled at him. 'That's a much better idea, isn't it, Kim?'

Mark indicated the way with his chin. 'You know where the gate is, Ella.'

9

Kim's sneakers sunk into the hardy grass. They followed him to the terrace.

'Want to come inside or sit here?' he asked them.

Ella said, 'The terrace is fine. It's nicely sheltered from the wind and we won't mess up your carpets.'

He nodded without a comment. 'What can I get you?'

Kim decided to say something before he thought she'd lost her voice. 'Whatever you're having.'

He lifted his mug in their direction. 'This is straight coffee, but I can offer you latte or cappuccino or espresso.'

Ella answered, 'Straight coffee will be fine.' Kim nodded in agreement.

Mark disappeared and they sat down. Kim looked around. There was a ship far out to sea, crossing the horizon where the sea met the sky. In a matter of minutes he returned with mugs, milk and sugar on a tray. He flopped into an opposite chair and stuck his long legs out in a straight line.

Kim said, 'It's a lovely house, Mark.'

'Yes, I like it too — even if I rattle around in all the emptiness most of the time. I couldn't maintain it properly if I didn't have Maggie Foster and her husband. She looks after the house and he battles with the garden. I'm thinking of selling it. It's a house for a family, not for a single bloke.'

The idea of him with a family produced a gamut of perplexing emotions in Kim and her stomach churned. She said, 'I understand that, but it's such a beautiful position. You'll have a job to find somewhere comparable.'

He eyed her thoughtfully. 'Yes, the views are spectacular, even in winter. Sometimes there's a non-stop parade of curious walkers in summer, but it's mostly very peaceful here.'

'The house looks very old.'

Tongue in cheek, he declared, 'Yes, it

even has a hidden passageway from the house down to the beach.'

Kim's eyes sparkled. 'Oh, how lovely! When I was a kid, I loved books where there were secret passageways or hidden rooms.'

'I came to play with some children who spent their summer holidays with their relatives,' Mark said. 'We had a great time. My parents lived further along the coast. My wife didn't like it because it was too cut off. She didn't like local weather much either, apart from the odd brilliantly sunny day in summer.'

Ella added, 'Well, she was a townie, so living here was a big contrast. Some people can't stand seclusion.'

He nodded and said wryly, 'Jill couldn't. I wish I'd known that before I bought the place. I always wanted to live here.'

'Your next neighbour must be Bill Saunders farther down the road,' Ella said.

'Yes. He tells me there are plans to

build some bungalows near here. I can get to Poole easily from here since they finished the new road passing the end of the lane.'

Ella nodded. 'Yes, I expect it makes a lot of difference. There was a lot of opposition at the time, wasn't there?'

Kim was still thinking about the secret tunnel. 'I presume the passage-way is well-hidden and the customs and excise people never found it?'

Mark looked amused. 'It is, but I bet they knew it was there. Perhaps the squire bribed them with money, or shared the booty to keep them quiet.'

'Is it hard to find?'

He laughed softly. 'Yes, unless you've a sharp eye. You're welcome to try your luck. It has a hidden entrance at both ends, so it's very important to know how to get out as well as how to get in. Otherwise, you'll end up as a skeleton. Do you know where it is, Ella?'

She smiled. 'No. I didn't know the people. There are countless secret doors and secret passageways locally. I'm not so easily impressed as Kim is.'

Mark asked Kim, 'How's business?'

'Customers aren't flooding in, but I'm not expecting to make much profit for a while. It's the wrong time of year.' He nodded and she continued, 'I've found a couple of interesting pictures among all the ones Uncle Bill hoarded upstairs.'

His eyebrows lifted. 'Really?'

'Ever heard of Martin Bunsworth or Ralf Hollister? I found their names on the internet. Nothing sensational, but at least they're known names.'

He shook his head slightly. 'They don't ring a bell with me, but if you've found references to them, that's good.'

'I'm thinking of showing them to someone with more knowledge. It'd be a good excuse for a trip to London.'

'When were they around?'

'The artists? They were popular at the turn of the century.'

'If you like, I'll find out who knows about that period. Oil paintings? English?' Kim nodded. 'Take my advice. Don't just turn up to get them checked. They'll throw you out with a flea in your ear. You need an appointment.'

'I know. I wouldn't go on the mere chance.'

Ella looked at her watch. 'We have to go. Tony and I are in the darts team and it's my turn to cook a meal before we go. I'm hopeless at darts but they need me to make up the numbers.'

Mark asked Kim, 'Do you play too?'

'No. They'd be lethal weapons in my hands. I can't aim straight.'

Ella said, 'Can't be worse than I am! Come, if you've nothing better to do. You already know Tony and me, and Anna too. It'll give you a chance to meet some more people from the village. What about you, Mark? You haven't been to the pub for ages.'

Mark looked almost regretful. 'Sorry, I can't. I'm leaving at the crack of dawn to go to Manchester. Next time, perhaps?'

Kim was surprised at how disappointed she felt.

Ella said, 'You'd better make an effort

soon, or people will call you stuck-up and arrogant.'

'I don't think that bothers him,' Kim said. 'I've already accused him of being patronizing, and it didn't make any difference.'

Ella laughed. 'Did you? Good for you!'

Mark held up his hands in defence. 'Two women against one man is not fair.'

They got up. 'Thanks for the coffee,' Ella said.

'Any time you want to search for the secret tunnel, Kim, let me know.'

She nodded but didn't think she ever would.

Mark walked with them as far as the gate and stood watching them with his hands in his pockets and his hair tousled by the wind, until they were out of sight.

Kim remarked, 'I'm surprised he's interested in what goes on in the village. He's very professional, proficient, and reserved. I bet he's been to a private school and university. I've met several men like him in the course of my work. They were always men who liked to be in charge and didn't care about what other people thought or did. That attitude wouldn't suit local people, would it?'

'Oh, he fits in and he cares about people he likes. He also has a very good sense of humour and he isn't snobbish. Underneath all that refinement, he's still the boy who went with us to the primary school. His further education was upper-class and private, but basically he's stayed the same. The collapse of his marriage shook him. I think Jill never understood him. She expected him to put her on a pedestal after they married and he didn't. She looked for someone who did.'

'Did you know her?'

Ella shrugged. 'She came to the pub with him a couple of times but it was obvious she didn't enjoy it. After a while he stopped coming, presumably because she didn't want to come.'

'He didn't come on his own?'

'Not until after her death, and even that was difficult for a while, because everybody avoided talking about Jill. He's adjusted now and pops in for an occasional drink, but he's always very busy.' Ella skipped over a large stone. 'Are you coming this evening?'

'Yes I will, if you think I'll fit in.'

'Of course you will!'

10

The following Friday, Kim met Tom on her way out of the grocery store. 'Coming tomorrow evening?' he asked her.

She smiled. 'Yes, I've been told all about the annual 'jig-about'. I'm supplying a potato salad.'

He nodded. 'It gives the village a chance to get together as a community. When the holiday season's in progress, people are too busy.'

'Yes, Ella explained. I think it's a good idea. A friend of mine is coming down this weekend. Ella said it's okay to bring him along.'

'Someone special?'

She shook her head and wrinkled her nose. 'Just the opposite. I thought he understood I didn't want to see him again. He didn't.'

'You should have been explicit. Then

you wouldn't have him as an unwelcome guest.'

She sighed. 'I know. I've only postponed the inevitable.'

* * *

Howard arrived first thing on Saturday morning. After a late breakfast, she introduced him to Audrey and showed him the gallery. Audrey raised her eyebrows and made a face when his back was turned. Kim had already told her about him.

Kim showed him some nearby attractions. He remarked that everything was very old-fashioned and behind the times. She managed to sidestep his arm and evaded him kissing her a couple of times. He clearly thought she was still interested. She had to sort that out over the weekend.

* * *

That evening, the community hall was decorated with paper streamers and coloured balloons. Pop music was blaring over the heads of people already chattering and dancing when Kim and Howard arrived.

Kim was glad to be among other people. Standing with her, Howard looked around and remarked, 'So, this is how the locals indulge themselves? This is their idea of fun? It's quite poignant. I haven't seen anything like this since my parents forced me to go to a street party years ago when I was a kid. I didn't think this was your kind of scene, darling.'

With heightened colour, Kim replied, 'Well, it is. There's no flashy sports centre, cinema, exclusive restaurant or disco around here. People are still more satisfied with their lives than most people I met in town.'

Sneering, Howard remarked, 'I wouldn't be surprised to find they fold the pavements up at six o'clock in this place. It's quaint.'

'You may not believe it, but they enjoy the peace and quiet.'

'I'd go barmy if I lived here!'

'No one is asking you to. I didn't think you'd understand. Your idea of fun is drinking yourself into a coma.'

'Hey, you never saw me that stoned.'

'I never saw you sober after a game of rugby either.'

He slipped his arm round her shoulder. 'Aw, come on. Don't spoil the weekend with bickering.'

'Evening!' Mark's voice broke in. 'I didn't expect to see you here, Kim.'

Kim smiled at him. 'And why not? I live in the village. Geographically you're the outsider, not me.'

There was a twinkle in his eyes. 'Touché. You're right. I always come to the annual do, otherwise people will lynch me.' He turned his attention to Howard. 'A new face in our midst? Hi, I'm Mark Fraser, and this is Gloria Turner.'

Kim saw that Howard thought these two were more to his taste. He stuck out his hand and Mark shook it. 'Howard Walton. Pleased to meet you.'

Gloria made no effort to give him her hand so he just dipped his head. 'Hello, Gloria.'

Kim was already fed up with Howard, and seeing Gloria at Mark's side didn't improve her mood either. The woman's elegant suit and bored expression didn't fit the surroundings. Kim's own dress was pretty enough, but not too trendy.

Mark looked at them speculatively. 'I presume you're Kim's friend?'

Howard hugged her shoulder and Kim knew she couldn't detach it without causing a scene, so she tolerated it in silence.

'Yes,' Howard said. 'She and I have known each other for ages.' Mark nodded. Howard looked at Gloria and although he guessed from her bored expression and stylish appearance that she didn't, he asked, 'Do you live here too?'

Her lips were slightly derisive. 'No, thank God. I'd shrivel up within weeks. I'm only visiting Mark.'

Mark shot her a look of irritation. 'You insisted on coming. I didn't force you, did I?'

Gloria coloured and played with her glass.

Howard said, 'I asked Kim how she manages to survive.'

Mark said, 'And what did she say?'

Kim answered, 'I said I like it here. It's the people who matter, not the attractions. Life is always what you make it.'

Gloria patted her French pleat. 'I suppose there's no accounting for taste.'

Kim wished Mark and Gloria would go away. Gloria eyed the gathering with obvious censure and she didn't bother with anyone except Mark. Kim decided to ignore her.

They watched the dancing and there was a tombola accompanied by a lot of commotion as the numbers were drawn. The music began again someone shouted, 'The Gay Gordon!' Tom and Ella were passing.

'Come on Kim, join in!' they invited her.

She laughed. 'I haven't danced the Gay Gordon since the sixth form.'

'Well now's your chance again.'

Ella challenged Howard. 'Come on, drag her into the circle with the rest of us.'

Howard's eyebrows shot up. 'Who, me? Are you kidding? I wouldn't take part in this if Robbie Williams in person was on the dance floor. It's for kids!'

A fraction of a second later, Mark grabbed Kim's hand. A prickle of excitement ran through her. He laughed. 'Come on, let's give it a whirl.'

The music started and the circle formed. They began to move back and forth, and to twist and turn. The laughter rang out as everyone demonstrated their existing or non-existent skills. Kim eyed Mark and was suddenly glad that she'd come after all. Either he was a first-class actor, or he was honestly enjoying himself as they cavorted around the floor. There were countless collisions but they kept going, as did everyone else. Some people eyed their progress and sent each other speculative looks. She was too busy keeping up and enjoying herself to notice any onlookers.

When the dance ended, she was slightly out of breath. Her cheeks were bright red. She looked at Mark and laughed. Her eyes sparkled.

He said. 'Gosh, I'm completely out of breath.'

'So am I.'

Still smiling, he held out the crook of his arm. Kim tucked her arm through his as if it was the most natural thing in the world. It felt right. They walked back to Howard and Gloria. Both of them were looking peeved.

Howard said, 'You looked like a couple of school kids, gallivanting around like that.'

Kim was annoyed. He was spoiling the evening for her. She'd had enough. She'd pampered him all day, to no avail. 'Howard, why don't you just go and watch TV, or perhaps you'd prefer to get in your car and drive home this evening? You don't like anything about Dulsworth, do you?'

Howard didn't like her snapping at him, especially when Gloria and Mark were bystanders. 'There's no need to get narked. Gloria said the same a minute ago.'

'Then Gloria should go somewhere else too.'

She turned and left them all standing. She thought she heard Mark chuckle. She went to talk to Tom and Ella and a group of other people from the village. Byron, who was a part-time fisherman and helped his father run the local pub, asked her to dance and she went willingly. Kim didn't care what the others were doing. She concentrated on enjoying herself. She liked the villagers. They were warm and friendly and had accepted her into their midst.

Later, she saw that the others had left. Gloria had probably persuaded Mark to leave. She wondered if Gloria was spending the night with Mark. The thought twisted and turned inside her. She hoped Howard had driven straight home.

When she got to the cottage, she was disappointed. Howard was watching the late-night sports show. She tried to stay calm.

He jumped to his feet when she came in. Throwing his arms around her shoulders, he said, 'Hi there, doll. Enjoy yourself?'

Kim squirmed out of his grasp.

He shrugged. With one eye still on the television screen, he asked, 'Why do you like this place? Living here would test the patience of a saint.'

She glared at him. 'You've been here one day. Does that make you an expert? I bet you don't even know the name of your own next-door neighbour.'

He held up his hands. 'I only need to know where to find the doctor when I need a sick note.'

'You're pathetic, Howard! This week-end was a big mistake. We've never been more than casual friends. We've nothing in common and there's no point in us seeing each other anymore.'

His lower lip jutted and he stated, 'You're right. If you intend to bury yourself in the country go ahead, but be careful you don't end up as a shrivelled and nasty little spinster.'

'I'll take my chances. You're not exactly God's gift to women. You're too self-centred and inconsiderate. Haven't you noticed that you've never kept a girlfriend for very long? Goodnight!' She turned on her heels and went upstairs. She didn't expect him to bother her but she locked the door anyway.

★ ★ ★

Neither of them had much to say next morning. Kim had already fetched the Sunday paper before Howard got up. He came into the kitchen with a sulky expression, sat down, and buried himself behind the sports pages while he ate. Finally, he slapped it down on the corner of the table and got up. He announced stiffly, 'I'm leaving to avoid the weekend traffic.' Kim didn't comment.

He packed his holdall and clattered downstairs again. Looking unenthusiastic, he avoided Kim's glance, hesitated, but did manage finally to say 'thank you' as he left.

Kim stood and watched with relief as his Japanese sports car tore up the hill. She was sure her next visitor would be a lot more welcome than Howard had been. He'd almost ruined her weekend.

11

Kim viewed the ledger. She should be satisfied, but she was still anxious. She needed a steady income to feel more secure. She chewed the top of her pencil and wondered how to promote more custom. Perhaps she was too ambitious too soon? The village was nowhere near a main highway, and visitors were generally tourists. She'd continue to offer low-priced aquarelles and gradually introduce some oil paintings. The income from the aquarelles provided the bread. Anything on top of that was the butter.

Hunting for pictures that no one else wanted, at auctions or from house clearances, would give her something to do besides waiting in the gallery. If she bought wisely and re-sold at a fair profit, she'd soon earn a good reputation. She began to flip through out-of-date specialist magazines stashed away in the cupboard.

Concentrating on the articles, she didn't hear the tinkle of the bell or the sound of Mark's feet as he came through.

He waited in the doorway for a moment. 'Hey, I could've emptied your walls unhindered.'

She looked up and her colour heightened. 'Mark, Hello. Yes, you're probably right. I was reading.'

He crossed to the table and looked down briefly at the periodicals spread over the surface. 'They're a bit out-of-date, aren't they?'

'I know, but the articles are still interesting and accurate. Uncle Bill must have had a subscription and then cancelled it because it was too expensive. They're four years old, but they're still relevant.' She decided not to discuss her plans. She'd softened her opinion about him, but there was no rational reason why she should bare her soul every time they met. His gallery in Poole specialized in modern art. They were worlds apart.

'I've piles of them at home — more

recent ones,' Mark said. 'You're welcome to them. I'll drop them off next time I'm passing.'

'Thanks, I'd be grateful. I'll return them of course. What can I do for you?'

'I've contacted a friend of mine about your paintings. The ones you wanted assessed.'

Disconcerted, Kim crossed her arms. 'Mark, what makes you think I need your help?'

He looked surprised and hesitated. With a slightly baffled expression, he said, 'I thought you'd be pleased.'

Looking at him, she needed a moment. 'Don't you think you should've asked first?'

He ran his hand down his face before he admitted, 'Yes, you're right. I just assumed you'd be glad.'

Feeling more amenable, Kim uttered, 'I know I don't have your contacts, but if I always depend on others, I'll never be a real art dealer.'

He nodded. 'Sorry, I didn't think you'd mind.'

The tenseness left her. 'I don't understand why you bother. You have enough
to do.' Kim gave him a shaky smile.

He was still uncertain, but he replied
calmly, 'I thought I'd cheer you up after
your troublesome weekend visitor finally
left.'

She laughed. 'Was it that obvious?'

'Did he leave the same evening?'

She took a deep breath and tried to
relax. 'No, not until next day, after
breakfast.' Her laugh sounded artificial
and he noticed.

'And you weren't sorry to see him
go?'

His gaze was so direct and disconcerting that it confused her. She didn't
understand why he made her feel so
nervous. She struggled and managed a
feeble answer. 'No, not a bit! I hope I
never see him again.' She looked up
into his face and found herself lost in
his eyes. She adjusted her thoughts and
asked, 'So, what have you arranged?'

'An old friend of mine knows a lot
about Victorian paintings, although he's

not a dealer. He works for an auction house. That makes him fairly neutral in his judgement.'

She nodded. 'Sounds good.'

'I explained that you needed an evaluation. He said he'd take a look at the paintings and tell you what he thinks. He said good photos will suffice for a quick judgement.'

'How can I contact him?'

He hesitated for a moment. 'I'm going up to London at the end of the week, and I suggested I'd bring you with me, and we'd meet Simon for lunch.'

She stirred uneasily in the chair but managed a smile. 'Fine. I can manage that, as long as it doesn't interfere with your business.'

He held her glance. 'Look, if you feel harassed, just say so. Simon won't mind if you call it off, and neither will I. I just wanted to help.'

Kim didn't understand why, but decided she should take advantage, especially when it didn't cost her anything. 'I don't feel harassed. If you've gone to so much trouble, I'd like to come. I'd just like you to check with me first before doing anything on my behalf in future, okay?' She gave him a tremulous smile.

He was clearly considering the situation. 'I'm used to making decisions without consulting anyone. I'm afraid I just didn't think about clearing it with you first.'

'When are you planning to go? I'll ask Audrey to take over for the day. It is just for the one day?'

'Yes. I have a meeting on Thursday, and that suited Simon. If it's okay with you, and you don't mind getting up at the crack of dawn, we'll be in London just after the rush hour. I'll get my business out of the way straight away and perhaps you'd like to fill in your time doing something else? We'll meet Simon at the restaurant for lunch, and after that, we can leave whenever we like. I'll get you home the same day, promise.'

She wavered for a moment, choosing her words carefully. 'I'm grateful that you've gone to so much trouble. Please don't think that I'm not but, in future, I'd prefer to make my own plans when I'm working. That's what the gallery is; it's my work.'

He stuck his hands in his pocket. 'And it's right for you to feel that way, I understand perfectly. I'm still glad that you've decided to come. I'll give you the exact time later in the week. I'll pick you up.'

'And I'll take the pictures. I presume your friend needs prints?'

'Yes, and mark them in some way, so you know what belongs to what. Clip them, mark them, rubber-band them, whatever helps you keep them apart.' He paused. 'I'll be in touch.'

With increasing confusion, she felt how his presence progressively disturbed and excited her. She couldn't decide if that was good or bad. She didn't want her emotions to whirl out of control. Kim was astonished by the feeling of fulfilment and pleasure she felt whenever he was around, even though he still surprised her. She nodded. 'Right! What about a cup of coffee?'

He shook his head and his smile widened. 'Must be off! A customer of mine arrives in Poole in an hour's time. A possible sale!'

'Then I won't twist your arm. Next time perhaps?'

He nodded and turned on his heels. Lifting his hand, he bent his head and exited through the door. He didn't look back and she was free to watch his departing figure.

* * *

Kim tensed when she got a phone call from Howard that evening. She hoped he wouldn't try to smooth their differences.

'Hi. I got home in record time.'

Still taken aback, she said, 'Oh, that's good.'

'Yeah, I even managed to get in an

extra training session on Sunday afternoon. We're playing Walston United next Saturday.'

'Good! Hope you enjoy yourself.' For the lack of conversation, she added, 'I'm going up to London for the day on Thursday.'

'Are you? Lucky you! I understand why you want to get away from that place for a while. I'd go raving mad.'

'Don't start that again. It's lucky you don't live here, and never will, isn't it?'

'Rather! Actually, I'm phoning because I've lost my mobile. Found it?'

'No. I haven't. Whose phone are you using?'

'It's Sandra's, aren't I lucky?' There was the sound of giggling in the background. 'I'll have to search my car. Perhaps it's fallen between something.'

'That wouldn't surprise me. Your car is a travelling junk yard.'

'Don't mock, babe! You are so cynical and derisive! Life is more than a draining board full of clean mugs.'

'As you never wash any mugs, that

means you're enjoying life to the full.'

'I am. You don't appreciate what you've discarded.'

Kim laughed. 'Sorry to disappoint you, but I don't regret a thing. We don't match. If I find your phone, I'll let you know.'

He sounded disgruntled. 'Okay. That's all for now.'

'Okay. Bye, Howard.'

12

It felt good to sit next to Mark and watch the sky slip from semi-darkness into daylight. It was almost like waking up with someone in the same bedroom. They didn't talk much, just the usual generalities about the weather, the amount of traffic, and last night's news. Kim felt relaxed and comfortable and he seemed hassle-free too. The soft sound of a morning programme with discussions and bursts of pop music filled any gaps.

They stopped halfway for breakfast, and by then they were both livelier. The snack bar was fairly empty. The formica-topped tables and unimpressive chairs weren't inspiring, but the food was good and the coffee was hot. Munching on a slice of toast, Kim cleared the corner of her mouth with her fingertip before asking, 'What are you doing today?'

Mark speared some bacon and egg, and paused with the fork in mid-air. 'A small gallery has found us some drawings someone in the USA wants. I'll try to buy them for a decent price, and then pass them on to him for more.'

'Why doesn't he buy them direct?'

He smiled lazily. 'Because I know where they are, and he doesn't. That's how I make my money. I pocket the difference.'

'So your customer never realizes more than one dealer was involved?'

He nodded. 'Sometimes the margin is small, sometimes it's more. It depends on how rare the item is, and how determined the customer is to own it.'

'Ever made a mistake and the customer refused to pay as much as you wanted?'

He cleared his mouth and took a sip of coffee. 'Yes, of course. We all make mistakes, but experience has taught me only to buy if I'm certain I can also sell it elsewhere. If everything else fails, I get it auctioned off.'

'So it's a bit a gamble?'

He shrugged. 'Yes, I suppose so, but I always calculate the risk. As long as I cover my overheads, I can enjoy the fun of the hunt. Something expensive always finds a buyer at the end of the day. I could insist on a contract but sometimes that frightens people off. Trading is often a question of trust.'

She leaned back. 'It still sounds risky.'

'I often make more money from half-a-dozen smaller deals, like the one today, than a prestigious one. In due course, people remember you and recommend you. You gain new customers and meet new sellers. What are you doing this morning? Going on a shopping spree?'

'No. I'm watching my pennies at the moment.' His brows rose, and she continued. 'I think I'll visit a couple of museums.' She didn't add she hoped to find some pertinent literature about the Victorian era. Museum shops were goldmines for specialist books and information.

He reached into his breast pocket and handed her a small card. 'That's the name of the restaurant, and my mobile number is on the back. I've arranged to meet Simon there at one o'clock.'

'I'll have to watch the time. It slips away once I'm inside a museum.'

'Agreed. Bookshops are the same, aren't they?' He looked at his watch. 'Finished? Or would you like something else?'

She shook her head and gathered her belongings together. 'No, let's go. I enjoyed breakfast very much. Thank you for the treat. I never bother with breakfast normally. It's never much fun on your own.'

'Yes, that's true. Cooking for one isn't much fun, is it, but it's better than eating out all the time.'

'I'll cook you a meal one day, to pay you back.'

He offered her an unreadable expression and said, 'That's not necessary, but I'm sure I'd enjoy that.'

*   *   *

Kim enjoyed herself and bought several relevant books about Victorian painters. She also allowed herself the luxury of a taxi to get her to the restaurant on time.

It was exclusive and she was glad she was wearing a smart pencil skirt and fitted jacket. There was an atmosphere of fashionable privilege and she gave a stiff-lipped waiter Mark's name. The waiter nodded and asked her to follow him.

He led the way to a cosy corner table where Mark was reading a newspaper. He folded it and got up. He broke into a friendly smile and her mood improved no end.

'You made it on time.' He took her paper bag with the books. 'Let's put that out of the way.' He deposited her bag in the nearby corner.

The waiter pulled out Kim's chair and she sat down.

Mark asked, 'What would you like? Simon is on his way. How about an aperitif? Sherry, a cocktail, whatever you like.'

She shook her head. 'Some sparkling water would be lovely. I'm thirsty.'

'A dry martini for me and sparkling water for the lady.' The waiter gave a barely visible nod and disappeared.

Kim relaxed and looked around. 'This is very impressive! Do you come here often?'

'Now and then. Sometimes I invite a customer to lunch. This place has an excellent chef and it is well known for its atmosphere.'

She nodded. 'I can believe that. I wondered if the waiter would check my credentials before he let me in.'

He chuckled. 'Charles is one of the old guard. He's quite soft under that frosty exterior.'

'He looks like they put him in cold storage every night to stiffen his backbone.'

The warmth of Mark's smile gave her a lovely feeling of satisfaction. He laughed.

Kim looked around. 'No, seriously. It's splendid here.'

'I'm glad you like it.'

Their drinks arrived. She avoided eye contact with the waiter and Mark noticed. He grinned and lifted his glass. 'Here's to us, and to business!'

'To us is enough at present. I can't pretend that I'm much of a business-woman yet.'

'You're doing okay. You have the right attitude.'

'I wonder if you'd say that when I tell you I'd be just as happy eating fish and chips!'

He laughed softly. 'Nothing wrong with fish and chips; I like them too. I'm sure there are dozens of newly rich people who yearn for fish and chips in newspaper, but they wouldn't admit it because it doesn't fit their image anymore.'

They were interrupted when a young-ish man joined them. Mark got up and offered his hand. 'Simon, you made it! That's good. How are you?'

'Fine, and you?' He looked at Kim and waited.

'This is Kim, the young lady I told you about.'

Simon had blue eyes and blond hair. Some strands flopped onto his forehead. He took Kim's hand and shook it briefly. He was dressed casually, but his clothes were clearly expensive. In comparison, Mark's charcoal-grey suit and conservative tie looked more formal, but he'd been to a business meeting.

They all agreed to enjoy the meal before Simon looked at Kim's photos. The food was delicious and filling. Everyone chose something different and Kim's main course was one of the best she'd ever tasted. The Dover sole seemed to melt in her mouth. The two men talked about various acquaintances and Simon's family, but Kim didn't mind. It gave her an insight into Mark's private life. By the time they'd reached the stage of coffee, all of them were beginning to feel indolent. Simon looked at his watch and reminded them of the purpose of their meeting.

'I've got to be back at work in half an hour, so let's have a look at these paintings, Kim.'

She rummaged in her bag and handed him the photos.

'Good.' He started checking through the photos. He viewed some briefly, so Kim guessed that they weren't worthy of much interest. He hummed and hawed now and then, and he took his time. 'I'm not an expert, but there are one or two very interesting ones.' He fished out two from the pile. 'These two in particular. This one looks like it's by a quite well-known Victorian landscape painter, and I'm almost certain the other one is by Howard Clayton. Ever heard of him?'

She shook her head.

'He spent most of his life travelling and painting portraits of the lesser nobility. His paintings are not comparable with other famous portrait artists of his day, but he was prolific, and his work fetches decent prices these days, when it's auctioned off.'

Her eyes brightened. 'Really? What sort of money are we talking about?'

'The landscape might bring anything between four and six thousand; the portrait might go for double that amount at the right auction.'

'Wow!'

'What did they cost?'

'No idea. My godfather bought the occasional picture from people out of sympathy. Apparently it was his way of helping someone in difficulty. He never recorded what he paid, just stacked them upstairs and forgot them.'

Simon gave a soft laugh. 'Good heavens! Want to sell them?'

'No, not at the moment. I have to think about it first. It's good to know I've something in reserve though, if I run into financial difficulties. What about the others? None of them worth anything?'

He shrugged. 'I think most of them would sell at the right auction. All together perhaps a thousand, or thereabout.'

Colour flooded her cheeks. 'Gosh!

That's more than I expected. Thanks for your help. It's good to know I've some untouched capital if times get harder.'

Simon smiled at her speculatively. 'If you do decide to sell them, get in touch and I'll find out which auction houses would be best for you.' He reached into his breast pocket and handed her his visiting card.

She took it, looked at Mark and smiled.

Mark lifted his eyebrows and commented, 'It was worth the journey after all, wasn't it?'

*   *   *

Simon left them to finish their coffee in leisure. Kim felt excited. The pictures were her business nest-egg in times of trouble. She stirred her coffee with a silver spoon and said, 'It's very kind of Simon. I'd like to repay him.'

'I'm sure Simon doesn't expect anything. Send him a Christmas card or join us down the pub for a drink next time. He hasn't given you any written expertise, just his opinion.'

'Does he visit Dulsworth regularly?'

'No, but he visits a great-aunt occasionally. When he does, he usually calls on the way back. I've known him since boarding school. He's a nice chap. I'll let you know next time he's around, shall I?'

She folded her pristine white serviette and put it on the table, then nodded. 'Please do. I haven't asked you how your deal went.'

'I'm happy with my earnings.'

'Then I presume I don't need a bad conscience about this lunch? Or will you let me share the bill?'

He threw back his head a little and laughed softly. 'No. I'm glad you came. Did you enjoy today?'

She nodded. 'Yes, very much.'

'Good. That's all that matters. Shall we try to dodge the heavy traffic out of town? If we leave now, we'll be home long before dark.'

'As long as you've finished your business. I don't mind waiting if you haven't.'

As an answer, he lifted his hand to gain the attention of the waiter.

* * *

The journey back was just as enjoyable. Kim liked being with Mark very much. He was intelligent and a mine of knowledge about all sorts of things. She kept up with his conversation and he looked at ease with her. He offered to stop for a meal along the way, but when she said she was still digesting her lunch and she wasn't hungry, he admitted he felt the same. They only made a brief stop for a drink. Daylight was fading by the time he steered the car down the road into the village. Outside her cottage, Kim got out and bent down.

'Thanks a lot, Mark. Not just for putting me in touch with Simon, but also for a really good day.'

'I enjoyed it too.'

'I'd like to invite you to a meal. We must sort a date out.'

'Something for me to look forward to. I'll think about it whenever I open a tin of baked beans!'

Kim laughed and slammed the car door. She waited until he drove off down the narrow street leading down to the harbour.

She opened the door and sighed softly. It had been a lovely day. Not just because of Simon's uplifting news about the pictures, but also because she'd spent a very enjoyable time with Mark. She reminded herself to be sensible and to be careful. Mark was a cultivated, polite man of the world and he was capable of turning her head without much effort on his part. His broken marriage had dented his faith in women but she didn't want to end up as a passing affair.

Kim couldn't figure out why he'd helped her. She had to be careful not to read too much into the situation. They were tentative friends. There was no need to expect more than his friend-ship. She was too sensible to be carried away by an impression. Just thinking about him was getting to be a dangerous habit.

She dumped the carrier-bag on the living-room sofa and went into the kitchen to switch on the kettle. She loaded the floral tray with the teapot and a cup and saucer. Staring out of the kitchen window at her own reflection, she wondered what was around the next bend.

13

Next afternoon Audrey asked, 'How did things go in London? Was there a masterpiece hidden upstairs?'

Kim shook her head. 'There are one or two good ones among them though.'

'Really? Not that I'm that surprised. I don't think your uncle was a bad judge of art. If he bought one he thought was rubbish, he threw it straight in the bin.'

'Ah, perhaps that's where the real masterpieces landed! Did he throw a lot away?'

'No, not many. Most of them landed upstairs.'

'It wasn't very good business policy, but he still kept the gallery going. His attitude didn't put him out of business.'

'Shall I make us a cup of tea? Ben is coming in this afternoon to fix the leaking pipe under the sink.'

Kim shook her head. 'Not for me,

thanks. Make sure Ben gets an extra portion of chocolate biscuits. He loves them. I'm so glad I don't have to pay someone for all these extra little jobs. I'm off to do my weekly shopping and to visit Adrian on the way. I'll go to that local house-sale on the way back to see if there is anything worth buying. I'm not sure if I'll see you before you leave but if not, I'll see you on Saturday.' She slung her bag over her shoulder and grabbed her coat.

Audrey pulled a magazine out of her shopping bag and went to put the kettle on.

* * *

Kim called on Adrian first. The day was grey and blustery. The coastal scenery didn't look so welcoming today, but it was still impressive. The cliffs looked completely different to the last time she was here.

She knocked the door loudly, in vain. After a minute or two, she lifted the latch. The door opened and she called Adrian's name as she went down the empty hallway. Adrian emerged from the back room and when he saw her, his face lit up.

'Kim! What a nice surprise!'

'I wanted to see my portrait. Made any progress?'

'Yes, come and have a look, although it's probably not advisable when it's only half-finished.' He held out his arm in a welcoming gesture and she tucked hers through his and joined him.

'I haven't given it exclusive attention, because Mark wants more still-life stuff to take to London next time he goes. It's over here.'

One easel stood in the centre of the room and various tubes of paints and his artist's palette lay on the nearby table together with rags and a variety of other things. On the far side in the shadows was another easel, and Kim went towards it with heightened interest. She could recognize the likeness. He'd captured her with a slightly wistful expression. 'Is that how you see me?'

'Yes; you're someone who likes to be private, but has to be public.'

She considered it silently. 'I quite like it.'

He laughed. 'That's praise indeed. How are things?'

'Not so bad. How are you?'

'Since Mark took me on, I feel great. The money from the sale of those pictures will keep my head above water for a while no matter what happens. So I'm free to paint without worrying how to pay for coffee.'

'How does Mark assess your chances?'

'He's quite optimistic.' He put his arm round her shoulders. 'Come and have a cup of coffee.' She let him guide her. He continued, 'He can't make a miracle happen, I know that. There are too many artists trying to break through. It might take time but he seems to think that I'll make it one day.'

Kim sat down at the kitchen table. 'I'm sure you'll make it to the top one day. You must be patient and keep painting. Mark is good at his job and he has the right contacts.'

Adrian put two steaming mugs on the rough wooden surface among the clutter and sat down. 'Yes. He's a tough businessman, but whenever I mentioned his name, people said he doesn't waste his time unless he thinks it's worthwhile. Want a biscuit?'

'No thanks.' She sipped her coffee. 'I went up to London with him the other day to show someone he knew Uncle Bill's other oil canvases.'

'And?'

'Nothing sensational, but one or two are worth something. Mark knows an awful lot of people, doesn't he?'

'Not surprising when one realises he's been in the business for years.'

Kim looked down at her mug. She was too curious not to ask, 'Did you know his ex-wife?'

'Yes. Not very well. I met her a couple of times when I was giving summer courses in the hotel. She seemed to spend a lot of time in the hotel bar. I even saw her there once with the chap she had an affair with. That was a pretty stupid place to go if she didn't want anyone knowing what was going on.' He shrugged. 'Perhaps it was intentional.'

'What was she like?'

He looked thoughtful. 'Beautiful, I suppose. Very exuberant, and she liked to be the centre of attention. I remember someone telling me that, in comparison, her husband was reserved. I noticed she flirted around in the bar, but I was too busy with my courses to be distracted by her goings-on.'

'So she was beautiful?'

'Um! And bored! She looked spectacular — pale blond hair, deep blue eyes, and an eye-catching figure.'

'If she'd had something sensible to do, she might not have gone looking elsewhere.'

He shifted in his seat. 'I don't think it would've made any difference. From what I saw, she needed the limelight and the good life. I've met several women like her; the pattern is always the same. They give nothing and expect the moon on a silver platter.'

'It makes me feel rustic.'

'Don't be silly! You're perfect as you are. You'd never be happy playing around and having meaningless affairs, Kim. You need solidity, reliability, trustworthiness.' He grinned. 'If you want to have an affair, let me know. I'll come like a shot.'

They chatted for a while about his work, the gallery and his hopes and dreams. He was the kind of person she'd have liked as a brother.

★ ★ ★

On her way to the supermarket, Kim thought about Adrian's comments. She felt sorry for Mark. She presumed he hadn't made his marriage vows without meaning them. Apparently, he and his wife weren't even compatible even before they married, but he wasn't the first man who'd noticed that too late. If she'd made an effort and occupied her time with something sensible, things might have been different.

She parked and stared ahead for a moment. Botheration! Why did it matter? She had enough to worry about in her own life. She didn't need to speculate about his.

★   ★   ★

After shopping, she went to the house sale. It was interesting. There were no oil paintings on offer, just some faded sepia photos, but it gave her an idea of what to expect. She'd decided to focus on Victorian pictures. It seemed to be a popular area, but perhaps local house sales might produce something now and then. She liked paintings of the countryside, especially ones with cows. She liked cows. There was something so endearing about them, and the Victorians seemed to like them too. She'd been reading up on it.

14

Sales slumped as autumn progressed. The weather didn't entice many tourists and things wouldn't improve till the springtime. Kim was sticking to Uncle Bill's methods of spreading his income to carry him through the year. Kim had already met the firm handling his bookkeeping and taxation. They told her Uncle Bill continually mislaid bills, payments, and sales invoices. He'd ended up paying too much tax because of it. Kim assured them that she'd keep a closer eye on everything.

* * *

One Sunday evening Kim was relaxing with an interesting book and a glass of wine. The weak autumn sunshine had disappeared long ago. She looked out of the window. The wind was grabbing at the remaining leaves on the old apple tree. The whole garden was slipping into preparations for winter. Daylight was fading fast. She got up and lit the fire in the grate. When it began to crackle and glow, she picked up her book again. These were the special moments she loved. This was her cottage, her home. The longer she lived in the village the more she felt that she'd found her niche in life at last. Uncle Bill had been right when he thought this kind of existence might suit her.

She looked through the window when someone knocked the door. Mark's car was parked on the road. Her heartbeat went faster but her voice was steady when she opened the door and said, 'Hello!'

The feeling of pleasure faded when she noticed Gloria by his side. Kim wondered if there was more to their relationship than people imagined. As the thought whizzed uncomfortably through her brain, she waited expectantly. Mark had a bundle of magazines in his arms.

'Hello, Kim. Here are the magazines I promised.'

'Oh, thanks! Do you want them back?'

He waved her remark away with a gesture. 'No. That's not why I'm here. I phoned Adrian this morning and persuaded him to come down the pub for a drink. I want him to meet Gloria. If we're representing him, it's sensible for him to know everyone who works for the gallery.'

Kim nodded. 'And?'

'I thought you'd like to join us. You know Adrian well. He might feel more comfortable with you around.'

'Oh! I won't make any difference. He's cosmopolitan enough to hold his own.'

'Perhaps, but I think it'd be nice to have you there. You were involved from the very beginning.'

Kim didn't fancy spending time with Gloria. She gestured towards the living room. 'I've just lit the fire. I'm planning a quiet evening with a good book.'

He glanced at her faded jeans, checked shirt and oversized teddy slippers. He grinned. 'You can put a guard in front of the fire, can't you?'

Sounding impolite, Gloria said, 'If she's happier with a book, leave her to it!'

As much as Kim wanted to ignore Gloria, her words prompted Kim to dampen her hopes. 'Oh, all right. Give me a couple of minutes to change into something else. Come in!'

Her reward was a slow smile. 'That's better.'

She didn't wait until they were inside. She headed upstairs. Minutes later, she returned wearing smart trousers and a turquoise cashmere pullover that had cost her more than she cared to remember. Mark and Gloria were waiting in the small sitting room. He was busy arranging the folding guard in front of the fire.

Gloria eyed the surroundings with interest. She walked towards a mirror hanging above an old carved chest, patted her hair and remarked, 'This is a nice little cottage. It would probably go for a bomb as a weekend retreat for Londoners, if you decided to sell it.'

Why did Kim get so annoyed every time Gloria opened her mouth? Coming from Gloria, the remark needled her. Kim straightened her shoulders. 'I love it. It's what I've always wanted — a home of my own. I've no intention of selling it, ever.'

'If you go bankrupt you might have to.'

'I don't intend to go bankrupt.'

Mark turned towards Kim. 'With your determination and attitude, I don't think you will. I'll leave the car here and we'll walk down to the pub, shall we?'

Kim wondered if Mark noticed she and Gloria hit sparks off each other all the time. 'How's Adrian getting here?' she asked. 'He doesn't own a car.'

'He's begging a lift from a friend, and I'll take him home after,' Mark replied.

'That limits your freedom to drink, doesn't it?'

He shrugged. 'That's okay. I can still enjoy company without getting smashed. I couldn't afford to lose my licence. My work depends on it.'

They walked down the hill. The wind was blustery and it tugged at their coats. The Sailor's Arms was busy. The old building had seen centuries of comings and goings. The blackened crossbeams were ancient, the fireplace was massive, and the horse brasses and farm implements on the walls were genuine. Cosy lighting rounded off a welcoming atmosphere. Adrian was already sitting in a corner. He waved his hand wildly to attract them. They made their way through the bustle.

'Am I glad to see you! I've been defending this corner for ages.' He patted the seat next to him. 'Come here, Kim. I need someone to keep me warm.'

Mark pulled back two farmhouse chairs with thick cushions and explained, 'This is Gloria. She's my Girl Friday. I thought it was a good idea for you to meet in less formal surroundings.'

Adrian nodded. He draped his arm casually around Kim's shoulder. She could smell turpentine mixed up with his aftershave. He wore new-looking chinos and a soft leather jacket — probably his best outfit. He was making an effort. Probably he wanted to demonstrate that he wasn't a run-down artist. Adrian dealt with lots of people through his painting courses; he knew how to fit in.

Mark asked, 'What's it to be?'

While he was at the bar, Gloria eyed them and said, 'Mark mentioned that you're painting a portrait of Kim?'

'Yes, I am. My idea, not his.'

She sounded almost interested. 'Have you seen it yet, Kim?'

'Yes. It is hard for me to judge, but I do recognize myself.'

Adrian grinned. 'I don't care what others think. I'm painting her as I see her, for my own pleasure.' He ruffled Kim's hair and she could only grin back at him.

Mark returned. He took off his

overcoat and flung it over a nearby bench. He looked good in toffee-coloured corduroys and a pale beige sweater. The others made small talk and Kim had time to study Mark without anyone noticing. She liked the combination of his dark hair, green eyes and lightly tanned skin.

He must spend a lot of time outdoors to have that kind of healthy colour. Perhaps somewhere among his ancestors there was someone from sunnier Mediterranean climes. She liked that idea. His business was near the harbour and his house overlooked the sea, so perhaps his tan wasn't surprising after all. Kim dragged her attention back to the present and found that he was telling them about Simon valuing Bill's pictures.

A brief shadow of annoyance crossed her face. She didn't like him discussing her business, even if it wasn't really important. She managed to sound friendly when she said, 'I'm sure Adrian and Gloria aren't interested.'

Mark hesitated. 'You don't mind me mentioning it, do you? I thought it was a stroke of luck, and well worth talking about.'

She shrugged. 'It's okay. They weren't sensational finds.'

Mark added, 'Not sensational, but something to fall back on for a rainy day.'

Gloria's interest stirred. 'How lucky! You'd better keep a close eye on them. It'd be easy to break into your gallery. A thief could help himself at leisure.'

Gloria didn't miss much. She must know her way round the gallery. Kim said, 'They're not there anymore. They're upstairs in the cottage.'

Byron came from behind the bar. 'I wanted to say hello to my favourite newcomer to the village. Hi, Kim!' He nodded to the others and gave Kim a kiss on her cheek. 'Hi, Mark! Don't see you in here very often these days.'

Mark viewed him. His expression gave nothing away. He smiled. 'I'm fine! How are you? I've neglected things but

I hope to start catching up again soon.'

Byron's father called him back to the bar. Nodding to everyone, Byron said, 'Back to the grindstone! Enjoy yourselves!'

Gloria shifted in her seat. 'Who was that?'

Mark obliged. 'You mean Byron? His father owns the pub.' He looked across at Kim. 'Is he still a fisherman?'

'Yes, I think the pub can't support the whole family, so until his dad retires, he supplements his income with fishing. He's nice.'

'A fisherman?' Sarcasm tinged Gloria's voice. 'You do know some colourful people, Kim!'

'Variety is the spice of life. What difference does it make what he does? Byron is a nice person. That's what matters.'

Mark added, 'I agree. He's the salt of the earth. We went to school together.'

Gloria looked down quickly and fiddled with the rings on her hand. She hastily asked about Adrian's painting career.

Kim had heard most of it before. She enjoyed the pub atmosphere and her thoughts were free to wander.

She'd promised to cook Mark a meal one evening. She wasn't sure how to approach it. What role did Gloria play in his life? He didn't mention Gloria in his conversation except in references to his business, but she was often with him. She'd need to make discreet enquiries beforehand. She didn't want to invite Gloria, but if they were a pair . . . Perhaps Audrey or Ella knew more.

Gloria was undoubtedly intelligent and good at her job, but was she right for Mark? She would bask in his name and connections, but she'd have to make a real effort to fit in locally. Would she do that? Kim hoped Mark wouldn't make the same mistake twice, even if Gloria did seem to idolize him. She looked at Mark and found him watching her too. His gaze was direct and disconcerting. Her feelings for him, whatever they were, were intensifying with every meeting.

Adrian watched them too, and reflected on the possibilities.

Kim concentrated on Adrian and Gloria discussing David Hockney. The evening passed quickly. When they decided to call it a day, Mark helped Gloria into her sheepskin coat and Adrian held out Kim's warm red duffle. They wandered up the hill to where Mark's car waited. Kim's hands were in her pocket. She hunched against the wind at the garden gate. She asked politely, 'Would anyone like a nightcap?'

Mark answered for them all. 'Not this time. I'm dropping Adrian off at his cottage and then taking Gloria back to Poole.'

Kim nodded and felt pleased that Gloria wasn't spending the night in his house. She steadied when she realized he could be staying overnight with her. The wind was rearranging her hair. She watched until his car's tail-lights disappeared from sight.

Back in the cottage there were still some embers glowing in the fireplace.

Kim threw on another log and thought about the evening. She'd enjoyed it. She even saw Gloria in a kinder light now that she'd at least shown interest in Adrian and his work. No one could dislike Adrian.

Kim liked Mark too. In fact, she liked him a lot. It wasn't sensible but sometimes logical behaviour flew out of the window. She hoped he thought of her as a friend but she wasn't sure. He was good at hiding what he felt.

15

Kim studied house-sale announcements in local newspapers and shop windows. She went to a couple. In one of them, she bought a Victorian painting. It was a scene of cows drinking at village pond. It was a popular Victorian theme and although the painting needed cleaning, Kim outbid someone else and still paid a very fair price.

When Kim brought it back to the gallery, she showed it to Audrey and Ben and explained how she intended to expand the variety of paintings on offer.

Ben stroked his chin and nodded. 'That's what this place needs — some new ideas.'

They helped her rearrange some of the paintings on the wall and hang her new acquisition in one of the niches.

That evening she created a simple

website for the gallery and included some photos of the paintings on offer. The website was part of her flat rate. Kim hoped that some interested party might find it.

* * *

Kim hoodwinked Audrey and Ella into talking about people in the village and eventually she manipulated them around to talking about Mark. Both of them said they hadn't heard any rumours about a romance. Audrey did speculate that Mark might have someone in London because he was there so often.

Kim decided it was safe to invite him for a meal. She phoned his home one day and left her message on the answering machine. She cleared her throat and said, 'Hello, Mark! Kim here. I promised you a meal. I'm visiting my sister next weekend. How about this weekend or in two weeks' time? If neither of them suit, perhaps you'd like to suggest something else? Hope you're well. Bye!'

The answering machine gave him a chance to make an excuse if he didn't want to come.

Kim was watching the television that evening when he phoned back.

'Hello,' he said. 'Thanks for the invite. Either date is okay. I try to keep the weekends free apart from the occasional Saturday morning in the gallery.'

'Good! What about this Saturday then?'

'Fine! What time?'

Feeling flustered by the mere sound of his voice, Kim replied, 'About six thirty, seven?'

'I'll be there.' He paused. 'How are things?'

'Okay. There aren't many visitors but it's a dismal time of year.'

'Things will improve eventually, I'm sure.'

'I hope so.'

'I'll see you on Saturday then.'

'Yes. Bye!'

'Bye!'

She stood with the telephone in her hand, staring into space.

* * *

The cottage was warm and cosy. That was the advantage of small rooms: it didn't take much of an effort to make them look good — lots of candles, bright cushions, a fire in the grate and the smell of cooking in the air.

As Kim expected, Mark arrived on time. She straightened her skirt and gave her face a quick inspection in the mirror on the way to the door.

The wind tangled his hair as he stood on the doorstep holding a bunch of flowers and a bottle of wine. She smiled and gestured him inside. He held out the flowers and the bottle.

'How lovely! Thank you!' She looked at the large bunch of narcissus and marigolds. The smell was strong and sweet. 'They're lovely.'

'I had no idea what sort of flowers

you like. I left it up to the shop owner to choose.'

'I love all flowers. I'll fetch a vase. Take off your coat and make yourself comfortable.'

She searched the broom cupboard for a vase. On her way back, she checked the oven and started the vegetables. Mark was standing in front of the fire rubbing his hands. The flames painted a golden pattern across his face. He smiled. 'There's nothing like a real fire. I'm afraid I don't make the effort very often. It doesn't seem worth the bother.'

Kim put the flowers on the window sill and tweaked them here and there until she was satisfied. 'Of course it's worth it. A fire is wonderful in the autumn and winter.'

He laughed softly. 'You're probably right. Goodness knows I have enough fireplaces. There are even some in the bedrooms. Thank heavens for central heating though, otherwise I'd freeze to death.'

She nodded. 'Well, the house is very exposed, isn't it?'

'Yes, the heating bills in winter are a nightmare. I can't do much about external insulation because of protection orders, but I've started insulating from inside whenever a room is redecorated.'

'Just keep in mind how the summer-time compensates you. It must be lovely to live there in summer. What would you like to drink?'

He tipped his head to the side. 'What about a glass of my wine? That's why I brought it.'

'Sounds good.' She handed him the bottle opener and fetched two long-stemmed glasses. After she took a sip, she said, 'Very refreshing! Just how I like it.'

His eyes sparkled. 'Good!' He looked around. 'I like your cottage. It's very comfy.'

'You'd probably end up like the hunch-back of Notre Dame if you lived here.'

'Lots of tall people live in cottages. It's all a question of adjusting to circum-stances, isn't it?'

'Had a good week? Please sit down. That chair is very comfortable.'

He did as she asked and she sat down in the opposite chair. His long legs stuck out in a long line and he leaned forward. The flames continued to flicker smidgens of gold across his face. 'Quite good! We had a customer who was a bit of a pain in the neck though. He wanted an etching for less than we'd bought it for. He needed convincing to make him realize we're not in business for fun. I'm not certain if he was just bluffing, didn't know the market price, or really thought his offer was fair.'

Kim laughed. 'Why didn't you just give up and tell him to take a running jump?'

He chuckled. 'I didn't have another interested customer.'

'How did you finally persuade him?'

'I told Gloria to take him out to lunch and persuade him. She convinced him it was a bargain.'

She looked down. 'So you made your profit?'

'A small one.' He cradled his drink and Kim got up.

'I'll just check on our meal.'

'It smells great.'

She put the final touches to the main course and picked up a small dish of appetizers. Coming back into the living room, she gestured him to the table. She deposited the appetizers on the rich cherry-wood table. She felt proud of its appearance — her best cutlery, glasses, white crockery, and a single white orchid in the centre.

Mark looked on with approval and sat down. 'This looks good.' He began to help himself and Kim relaxed. She was too nervous to eat much, but he made up for that. He drank sparingly and lifted his glass in her direction.

'Thanks for the invitation.'

She smiled and leaned back. She was glad that he'd come.

He rummaged through Kim's CDs when she went to fix the main course. He chose a piece of classical music that she'd always loved and it provided just the right background as they ate. The mustard-stuffed chicken and vegetables turned out really well and he praised her efforts.

Their conversation wandered back and forth across various subjects, and Kim found they had a lot in common. The inevitable difference of opinion did crop up now and then, but neither of them was worried about that. They dawdled and chatted. When Kim said it was time for a dessert, Mark said, 'I'm not sure if I can manage any more.'

She'd made individual apple tarts and served them with whipped cream. He managed two, lifted his brow and said, 'I take that back. I love apple tarts.'

She laughed. He helped her to clear the table. She shooed him into the living room. He settled and added another log to the fire. She joined him with the rest of the wine.

He held out his glass. 'I can afford one more glass, and thanks for that meal. It was perfect.'

She coloured. 'My pleasure. I quite like cooking when I have time, but it isn't much fun cooking for one, is it?'

He leaned back. 'Not unless you're an enthusiastic cook. But sometimes hunger drives you to knock up something more than a frozen pizza, doesn't it?'

'I've got into the habit of making large portions and freezing part of it.'

'Good idea, but I rarely cook in the week. I'm happy if I manage something on the weekends.'

Kim made herself comfortable in the opposite armchair and told him about her idea of buying and selling Victorian paintings, and how she'd set up a website to attract customers that way.

'Hmm! A website as a selling platform is time-consuming. You'll have to fiddle with it after every sale. Any luck so far?'

She shook her head.

'Don't expect too much feedback. You'll be lucky to find a customer that way. There are millions of websites, and thousands of them deal with art. I've heard of people who invested too much time in internet trading. It isn't as easy as it seems.'

'I know that, but it didn't cost anything to set up the site. Other permanent advertising is expensive. I can always re-vamp it if it gets too uncontrollable. Do you have a website?'

'Yes, but it's a simple one. It only introduces the gallery in pictures, tells people how to find us, offers enquiry and email facilities, telephone numbers, that sort of thing. Most of the time we deal on commission, so a complex website that needs continual updating wouldn't be much use to us.'

She looked a little downhearted.

He leaned across and met her eyes. 'It's not a bad idea, Kim. I just mean you shouldn't expect wonders. It won't bring a bevy of customers banging on your door overnight.'

She straightened. 'I didn't expect it would. I just want to try anything that might attract more customers.'

'You're doing fine. Come next spring, trade will improve, and if you manage to sell the odd painting in the gallery, by word of mouth, or through the internet before then, that's just fine.' He changed tracks. 'Seen Adrian lately? I haven't been in touch since we met down the pub.'

'He called in at the gallery one afternoon last week. He's still busy painting. Any interest, or chance of you finding someone to finance an exhibition in London?'

'People are interested, but there are so many budding artists trying to make it to the top. It takes patience. I do my best. I've told him that. You need to catch the eye of the right person at the right time.'

'I'm glad that you've taken him on. I know that he's grateful.'

He shrugged. 'I'm in London often and have a lot of contacts. He has talent. Are you planning any new exhibitions with someone else?'

'Not at the moment. Perhaps I'll put

one on again when the holiday season is in full swing. I still have a few of Uncle Bill's interesting pictures stacked away. If no one has discovered Adrian by then, he'll probably even agree to let me organize another one of his exhibitions.'

'By the way, you need better safety locks in the gallery. You don't have valuable stuff, but it might still attract a delinquent.'

She sighed. 'I know, but it's all extra expenditure. Uncle Bill never had any trouble.'

'That doesn't mean it won't happen. You're keeping those important paintings here in the cottage?'

'Yes. In the spare bedroom. I don't have extra security here either, but anyone who wanted to pinch pictures would try the gallery before this place.'

The logs had burned down and the embers glowed brightly. She reached forward to add a fresh supply. Mark reached forward and touched the back of her hand to stop her. His touch sent her emotions spiralling.

'It's gone midnight. It's time for me to go. It's been a great evening. You make your guests feel very comfort-able.' He smiled and her heart skipped a beat.

She didn't try to delay him. She smiled back. 'That's not difficult, when my guests are uncomplicated.'

He claimed his coat and knotted a red scarf around his throat.

Taking her hand in his, Kim only registered the gesture with confusion. She drew a breath to say something but before she could utter a word, he bent his head and brought his mouth down to hers. It was so unexpected that her lips parted beneath the pressure and a feeling of pleasure flooded through her being. It was brief and he gazed at her for a moment before he kissed her again more hungrily. Her heart thumped wildly and she wanted to cling to him. Her insides wanted more. He stepped away quickly and opened the door. She reasoned that perhaps a kiss like that might mean nothing to someone like

Mark. The cold air rushed at her and she didn't know if her lips were paralysed by the cold air or by the effect of the unexpected kiss. Water dripped from the low roof overhanging the doorway onto his shoulders. He stood for a moment, silhouetted by the street lighting.

His voice sounded deeper and thicker. 'Goodnight.' He bent forward and his lips found hers again. His kiss was hungry and Kim took what he gave gladly and wanted more. He lifted his hand and stroked her hair away from her face. The gesture was almost possessive. She presumed he wasn't the type to give any woman the impression he wanted more than friendship unless he really did.

'I'll be in touch. Take care, Kim.'

She nodded at him and must have looked like a startled teenager.

He turned on his heel, giving her no chance to say anything else. She couldn't have answered anyway. The only thing in her mind was the memory of how his kiss had affected her. Perhaps it was merely a polite gesture. Who knew what women among his circle of friends in London expected?

For her it was special. She'd never experienced such an intense feeling or longed for more. She already knew that she liked him, but there was something more, something magnetic about him. With thoughts whizzing through her mind, she watched him get into his car. She tried to come down to earth. His failed marriage was bound to make him cautious. Even though she realized it, she felt elated that he'd kissed her just now. She waited until he was out of sight. She shivered and closed the door. Leaning against it, she let her fingers travel over the surface of her lips.

*   *   *

Some days passed before Kim saw Mark again. She was in the garden raking the dried leaves that had blown across the patch of lawn and the flowerbeds.

She enjoyed the physical exercise as the pile of wrinkled beech leaves grew. He got out of his car and came to the fence. A slow smile spread across his face. Kim's immediate thought was that she wasn't looking her best in her oldest jeans, a washed-out windcheater and green wellingtons. He didn't seem to notice.

'Fighting the elements?' he asked her.

She coloured and couldn't keep the pleasure out of her voice. 'I'm trying. There's no wind today, so it's a chance to clear the garden before the really cold weather starts. I've never done any gardening before so I hope I'm doing this right.' She hoped she didn't sound too infantile. She was having trouble looking at him and ignoring the memory of his kiss.

'I don't have a problem with a lot of leaves because the garden is open to the elements and wind takes care of most of it.' He paused. 'When I saw you, I just remembered you told me you were visiting your sister in London. When are you going?'

'Next weekend. Why?'

He smiled an indolent type of smile. 'I'll be there then too. I've just had an invitation to an exhibition next Sunday. Is your weekend booked out, or have you time to come with me to an exhibition on Sunday evening? That's if you'd like to, of course.'

The cold air had already whipped colour into her cheeks; they grew rosier. 'I don't honestly know what's planned yet. I'm going up on Friday afternoon. My sister and I won't stop talking for hours, so Friday is full.' His eyes twinkled and he nodded. 'Then my parents are coming on Saturday and we're celebrating my brother-in-law's birthday. They stay overnight and leave after breakfast on Sunday. Usually everyone collapses after that. I intended to come back Sunday evening, or first thing Monday morning.'

'That means you could go with me on Sunday evening, then? I'd enjoy it much more in your company.'

'I don't know enough about art.'

'It's an exhibition. It's not a competition about how clued-up you are. Most of the people who go know nothing about art. They just want to be seen. Think about it! You have my mobile number. If you have time and would like to come, just phone me.

She nodded mutely.

He smiled. 'Good. Enjoy the gardening. I'm off to persuade a customer that a painting in my possession is what he's been looking for all his life.' He lifted his hand and got back into his car.

Kim continued to rake the leaves into piles with increased energy, and then stuffed them into plastic bags. Confused thoughts rushed around her brain. She told herself that his invitation didn't mean anything special. He was being polite. Perhaps he'd arranged to go with someone else who'd called it off, and he didn't like going on his own. The fact that she happened to be in London was just fate.

Kim didn't want to appear too willing. She'd play it by ear. Shelley might have already organised something for Sunday evening, and then going out with Mark would fall flat. She saw her sister and brother-in-law too seldom to give Mark precedence. Stacking the plastic bags alongside the wall to dispose of later, Kim went inside the cottage. After a shower, she'd go through the pile of local papers she'd collected all week, searching for any house-sales or local auctions that might be of interest. Perhaps that would divert her thoughts elsewhere for a while.

16

Kim's sister had taken the day off. The two women were different characters, but they still fell into each other's arms with hugs and kisses.

Kim looked around. 'Where's my favourite brother-in-law?'

'At the shop of course.' Dragging Kim along into the kitchen, Shelley made them coffee. Kim sat on a high stool at the breakfast counter and watched her sibling.

'You look tired. Everything okay?'

Shelley nodded. 'Of course. We're very busy at work at the moment.' She fidgeted with the coffee machine and avoided Kim's eyes.

'Hey, there's more to it than that, isn't there? I know you too well. Your determined expression has dents. What's wrong? Argued with your boss, or with Roger?'

Impatiently, Shelley replied, 'No of course not. Don't be silly!'

'Well? What is it then? Don't pretend everything is hunky-dory.'

'Damn it! You notice everything. Roger and I are fine, but we have a problem.'

'And . . . ?'

Shelley played with her hands nervously. 'We decided a while back we wanted children and nothing's happened. We've been married five years and trying for three of those. At first, we thought we just had to be patient.'

Kim's eyebrows rose and she tried to formulate comforting words. 'Sometimes pregnancy doesn't clock in automatically. I worked with someone who gave up trying. She and her husband started adoption proceedings and then she got pregnant!'

Shelley said sharply, 'I've heard all those kinds of stories, but I want to enjoy children when we're still young.'

'Quite honestly, I'm surprised that you want children. Roger would make a super dad, but you were always career-oriented. I thought children were a no-go area.'

'A marriage without children works for people who won't miss them. I think Roger and I might end up believing our time together was pointless without them. He loves kids and it'll surprise you to know I do too. Everyone thinks my job is the only thing I care about, but that's not true. I can organize my life to include children and I love Roger. He's taught me that life is more than balance sheets and reports. I'm prepared to step back, or even step down. The bookshop can support us both. Roger is very good at attracting customers and keeping them. People continue to buy from him, despite the internet and e-books. This flat, and everything in it, is paid for. I'm sure I could even work from home if we needed more money.'

Kim smiled. 'I'm glad. A baby is a wonderful idea. Is there a physical problem of some kind?'

'We haven't gone down that road yet,

but we do have an appointment to get checked out.'

Kim hesitated. 'If the result is negative, will you adopt?'

'I'm not sure. We've agreed to cross that bridge when we get to it.'

'You'll be ridden with guilt if it's your fault. I know you.'

'I'll take whatever comes.' She gave Kim a warning look. 'Don't you dare mention a word to Mum, or anyone else. I'll cut your favourite undies into shreds if you do. Don't show Roger that we've talked about it either!'

'No, of course not.' Kim slipped from the stool and went around the counter to give her sister a hug. 'Keep me posted. I'm there if you need someone to talk to. I don't want to intrude, but it might help. I'm always there for you, even though you often drive me completely crazy.'

Shelley gave her a shaky laugh and hugged her back before she busied herself at the sink again. With a thick voice, she said, 'Biscuits?'

They went to Roger's bookshop after doing some shopping. Kim had always loved Roger's old-fashioned set-up. The bookshop had wooden shelves and quiet corners with convenient armchairs for browsing. Roger had established a small bistro section in the area looking out onto the high street. The tables were all occupied with people enjoying a cup of coffee.

Roger emerged from behind the counter and gave Kim a hearty kiss and a welcoming smile. 'My favourite girl.'

'Hey! What about your wife?'

'After my wife of course.' He gestured towards the tables. 'What do you think? Be honest.'

'I like it. Anything that attracts customers is a good idea.'

'I think so too. How's your gallery? I'm looking forward to seeing it.'

'Shelley gave me her seal of approval when she made a flying visit, so I'm happy. I'm hoping trade will pick up when the holiday season starts.' Kim mused that a cafe in one of the upstairs rooms would work. She could share profits with the local baker. People might stay longer and look at pictures. It would bring in some extra cash.

Roger fetched them coffee and they caught up on each other's lives. They went to a local restaurant after Roger closed the shop. Delicious Italian food rounded off the evening to perfection.

*　　*　　*

Next morning Kim's parents arrived. After a late, drawn-out breakfast, the women began preparing food for that evening. Roger closed the shop punctually for once, to be home when his father arrived. His mother had died a couple of years previously.

The birthday celebration was warm and friendly, with family and some of Shelley and Roger's friends. The flat was full; the background music, food and wine were perfect; and everyone had a good time.

After a lazy breakfast next morning, Kim's mum and dad left. Roger spread himself across the couch with the Sunday newspapers and the women cleared the kitchen. While they were talking, Kim mentioned Mark's invitation to the art exhibition.

'Who's Mark?'

Kim explained and tried not to signal he was someone special.

'Sounds like he's an interesting man. It's about time you met somebody worthwhile.'

'Yes, he's interesting and nice but . . . '

'But what?'

'He's a widower. His ex-wife drowned before the divorce was settled.'

Her sister studied her carefully. 'You like him, admit it!'

'Yes, I like him. We're just friends.'

'Have you been out with him?'

'A couple of times; nothing romantic.' She ignored the memory of his kiss on her doorstep.

'As long as he's a decent chap, let

things take their course.' She stacked some dishes in an overhead cupboard and went on, 'What about that artist bloke? The one who called when I came down?'

'Adrian? Adrian is a good friend. There's no romance involved. He's painting a portrait of me.'

'Gosh! How posh! A genuine portrait by a real artist? So are you going to contact him?'

'Mark? I don't know.'

'Go! I went to one before I met Roger. It seemed to be an excuse for arty types to get together.'

Kim continued to dry the dishes. She stared out of the window at the park directly opposite.

'Ask him round for a drink beforehand.'

'He doesn't drink if he intends to drive.'

'Then I'll give him lemonade or tap water. Go on! I can tell you like him.'

Kim nodded. If he'd made other arrangements, she'd leave for home this afternoon.

She went to her room. Her throat was dry. Mark's mailbox told her he was unavailable at present. She felt a stab of disappointment, but fate had decided.

Back in the living room again, she said, 'He's not there. I think I'll catch the three-thirty this afternoon.' She'd barely finished when her cell phone rang. It was Mark.

'Kim? Sorry I missed you. I was out getting newspapers. Will you come?'

'Yes, if the offer's still open. My sister would like to invite you for a drink beforehand, if you have time.'

'Yes, Why not? We don't have to arrive at any particular time. These affairs are usually very formless. Ever been to a similar kind of thing?'

'No. I've only ever been to one exhibition — the one I organized for Adrian.'

He laughed softly. 'You won't get cider tonight. Tell your sister I'll be delighted to call. What time and where?'

She gave him the address. 'Is seven okay?'

'That'll be fine. See you then.'

'Bye!'

She looked up and Shelley gave her a thumbs-up sign. 'What are you going to wear?'

17

Kim could tell Shelley was impressed with Mark. He asked about Shelley's work and even knew someone who worked in the same company. Roger was more cautious, but Mark passed muster after they had a discussion about a recent best-selling political biography. Kim was uneasy about whether Mark felt happy with the situation.

They all chatted about the London theatre scene, or rather the other three did. Kim remained silent. She was glad when Mark looked at his watch. 'We need a taxi. It's time to be on our way.' He searched for a number stored in his phone.

Kim got up. 'I'll get my coat.' When she returned, Mark was thanking everyone. They left and found it was very cold outside.

'The taxi should be here soon. They said less than ten minutes.'

Kim nodded. 'No problem. I hope you didn't mind meeting my sister and her husband? That you didn't get the feeling they wanted to check if you're respectable enough.'

He laughed comfortably. 'No, it's fine. I understand perfectly. They're nice, your sister and her husband. Oh, here it comes!'

He tucked her arm through his as the taxi drew into the kerb. He handed her in and joined her.

★　★　★

The gallery was in the West End. The buzz of laughter and chatter drifted towards them as soon as they entered. Mark lifted his brows, looked around, and held out his hand for Kim's coat. She waited until he'd hung it on one of the overflowing clothes hooks. Putting his hand under her elbow, he raised his hand to greet some people he knew as they moved into the throng. Kim tried to see the pictures on the walls. They were very modern and painted in variations of red, black and white. She couldn't imagine what they symbolized, but she didn't waste time wondering. Modern art was modern art.

Mark grabbed some long-stemmed glasses of champagne from a side table, handed her one, and they came to a halt. His smile and his nearness confused her. She struggled with her inner uneasiness and was reluctant to admit he was the one and only reason she was here. A hidden voice warned her to be careful. He could be involved with another woman? Why did she go on believing in fairy-tales and in love-ever-after? It was wrong to hope for too much.

'What do you think of it?'

She looked around. 'No one is looking at the paintings. There are too many people. And I'm glad we came. It's a new experience.'

'Some are genuinely interested but

the majority are only here because it's fashionable.'

Someone slapped him on the shoulder. 'Mark, old chap! How are you? Haven't seen you for ages.'

'Hi, Jeffrey. I'm fine, how are you?'

'Okay.' He looked with interest at Kim. 'Who's this then?'

'Kim.'

'And what do you do for a living, Kim, besides being beautiful?'

'I try to sell paintings in a small seaside town.'

'Aha! That's the connection!'

With a good-humoured smile on his face, Mark said, 'I suppose so.'

Kim asked, 'And what do you do?'

'I restore paintings. It's a rickety job. I either have too much to do, or nothing. When I have nothing to do, I come to exhibitions with my wife Wanda. The drinks are free; I sometimes meet old friends, and get an offer of a job. Where'd you get those drinks?'

'From over there.'

'Be a good chap and get us a couple.

I'll introduce Kim to Wanda. She's by a potted plant, over there.'

With a bland expression, Mark nodded. He went, handing Kim his glass before he left.

Jeffrey turned away, expecting Kim to follow him. She did, guarding their glasses as best she could on the way.

Wanda was a neat dark brunette. Tiny curling tendrils escaped from her braided hair. Her dress was an understatement of elegance. Either Jeffrey made a lot of money from restoring pictures, or Wanda had her own income. Jeffrey introduced them and explained Kim was with Mark.

Wanda studied her carefully and said, 'I can't remember Mark bringing anyone since his wife died. Are you a serious twosome?'

'No, we're just good friends.'

'Ha! I've heard that somewhere before. It'd be good to see him with a decent girl again. His wife was completely wrong for him and he avoided people for a long time afterwards. There's his assistant, of course. What's her name? I've forgotten. All smiles and bottled hair.'

Kim was helpful. 'Gloria?'

'Yes that's it, Gloria! He brought her with him to a couple of business meetings. I suspect she fancies him but she's too brittle. She's not right for him. She wouldn't make him happy.'

Jeffrey butted in. 'Wanda darling, have you considered the possibility that Kim and Gloria are friends? They're both in the art business in the same area.'

'Are they? What difference does that make? I'm saying what I think. I thought you knew there's no point in trying to gag me?'

Kim laughed. 'I don't know Gloria very well. You can say what you like. I'll be as silent as the grave. Are you in the art business?'

'The same line as Mark,' Wanda replied. 'We're both salespeople, trying to sell stuff.'

Kim studied a picture on a nearby wall. 'Do you sell modern art like this?'

'Sometimes. I'll try to sell anything, as long as I get paid for doing so.' She considered Kim carefully. 'What do you think of this lot?'

Kim sensed she could be honest. Wanda was a woman who called a spade a spade. 'I know nothing about modern art, but I don't particularly like them. I can't imagine what they're supposed to be. They all look alike after a couple of minutes and the restriction to just three colours is boring.'

Wanda's laughed pealed out. Mark came, laden with glasses, and he handed Wanda and Jeffrey one each. He relieved Kim of the wrong glass. It was hers but she didn't make a fuss. He took a sip. She only mused how intimate it was for his lips to be where hers had been a moment ago. Perhaps the champagne was going to her head.

Mark said, 'Hi, Wanda. What are you laughing about?'

'Your friend. Kim's the first person I've met tonight who says exactly what she thinks.'

'And?'

'It was damning. I'm told this artist is

the find of the season, but she thinks he's rubbish.'

Flustered, Kim tried to defend herself. 'I didn't say he was rubbish. I just said I didn't like the pictures.'

Mark viewed her indulgently and shrugged. 'I won't comment. I know him.'

Wanda chuckled and lifted her glass. 'I like you, Mark!'

He lifted his glass to her. 'It's mutual, my dear! You know that.'

'You're one of the few people in the art dealers' world that I can stand.'

His expression was open and without deceit. 'That's because I never got into the habit of lying about, or cheating colleagues, although I was often tempted.'

Kim guessed Wanda liked him.

They stayed with Wanda and Jeffrey. No one seemed to bother about the pictures, but perhaps that was normal. A short time later, Simon and his girlfriend joined them. Simon pecked her cheek and nodded to Mark. Simon's girlfriend was a pretty blond with a heart-shaped face. She was quiet and intelligent.

After a while, somebody suggested a nearby nightclub. Mark looked at Kim quizzically. She shrugged and he agreed. Shadows blanketed the interior. Intimate tables stood in small niches. They all enjoyed themselves. There was a small space in the centre for dancing, but no one danced. Kim was glad. She didn't know how she'd react if she was in Mark's arms. He might look into her eyes and see her soul.

It was late when Mark grabbed a passing taxi. They said a quick goodbye to the others and the journey went fast, because the roads were quiet. When they'd almost reached Shelley's flat, Kim said, 'Thanks. I enjoyed every minute. I like your friends.'

Shadows flashed across Mark's face as they travelled along. 'Good. They liked you too. When are you going back home?'

'Tomorrow morning. Straight after breakfast.'

'I'm meeting someone tomorrow

morning, otherwise we could travel back together.' Kim felt a smidgen of disappointment. He went on, 'If I complete the deal fast, I can leave tomorrow evening.'

The taxi slowed down and drew up to the pavement. Kim said, 'Have a good journey when you do.'

When the taxi stopped, Mark got out to take her to the door. They stood in the shadows of a protecting overhang. He leaned forward and kissed her. At first it was just a lingering kiss, but then his mouth covered hers hungrily and was full of urgency and discovery. She immediately felt her body responding and he noticed it. She felt his uneven breathing on her face and then he pulled back. Holding her arms for a moment, there was tension in the air.

He said, 'I shouldn't have done that. I keep telling myself that if I kiss you it can't get better, but it does.' He traced his fingertip across her lip.

Feeling bemused, she replied. 'Is that so bad? I feel the same way.'

'Perhaps it's just my over-active imagination.'

Kim swallowed hard. 'About what? Sometimes we have to trust our instincts.' She hoped he'd tell her if there were other girlfriends or someone special, but he didn't.

The taxi blasted its horn. His brows wrinkled. 'Damn it! You mystify me and you rock my ordered existence.'

'Do I? Not intentionally! That's how life is.'

The taxi sounded the horn again.

She smiled shakily and was glad of the shadows. 'I think you'd better go. The driver's already annoyed.'

He nodded and bent to kiss her cheek briefly before he turned away. 'I'll be in touch.'

She wanted more of him but she fumbled in her bag for the key. Without another look in his direction, she hurried inside.

* * *

Shelley and Roger were already in bed.

Mark's kisses set Kim's insides on fire and she wanted him like she'd never wanted anyone before. It looked like he felt uncertain about her; perhaps he just had physical needs. She sighed and swallowed hard. She couldn't settle for an affair. Her heart wanted more than a fling between the sheets followed by misery. She looked in the mirror, removed her make-up and brushed her hair. There was nothing special about Kim Spenser. Mark knew a lot of beautiful, sophisticated women.

18

Kim hadn't slept well. Shelley asked, 'Did you enjoy yourself?'

Kim nodded. 'It was interesting. I met a couple of Mark's friends. We went on to a nightclub.'

Shelley looked satisfied. 'I like him. He looks good and he's the sort of man one can trust. I have to go! I'll phone this weekend. Have a safe journey. You can enjoy a leisurely breakfast.'

Kim stretched her arms above her head. 'No, I'm finished. I'll catch an earlier train. Thanks for a lovely weekend, and good luck with the tests.'

* * *

Kim stared at the passing scenery and tried to figure out why she liked Mark so much. He was friendly and interesting, but that wasn't why. He wakened something deeper in her, something she'd never felt before: a magnetic pull that she couldn't resist.

She drove her car from where she'd left it at the station. Dragging her case behind her, she walked up the path while searching for her key. She didn't need it. The door was open.

She paused and her mouth went dry. She decided to fetch someone else. No one was in sight so she walked down to the harbour. Byron was unloading some nets and floats from a ship next to the quay. Slightly out of breath, she explained. He left everything and came back with her.

They pushed the door open carefully. Once inside, Byron closed it quietly and told her to stay behind him. They went from room to room. Downstairs nothing seemed out of place. Following him up the narrow staircase, the main bedroom seemed untouched, as was the guest room. The smallest bedroom had a single bed but Kim mostly used it as a kind of box room. She immediately noticed the paintings she'd stacked against one of the walls were gone. Every single one.

She was shocked. 'The paintings! They've stolen my paintings!'

Byron looked puzzled. 'You had paintings in here?'

She nodded dumbly and explained, 'They were Uncle Bill's. I only brought the best ones here. Most of his stuff is still stacked upstairs in the gallery.'

He whistled. 'How many are missing? The police will want to know.'

'The police? Oh, yes. I suppose we have to call them.'

Byron nodded and looked around. 'It's strange, isn't it? Whoever did it didn't take anything else. They didn't damage anything either. It looks like the paintings were the only attraction. Let's make some tea and put a drop of something stronger in it! You look like you've seen a ghost. I'll phone them.'

Downstairs, Kim made a pot of tea while Byron rang the police. She listened as he explained what had happened. He came to sit at the table with her. 'They're sending someone as soon as possible.'

She nodded and pushed a cup and saucer across the table. 'I can't thank you enough, Byron.'

'I'm glad you were sensible and fetched me before you went inside. They could have been here.'

She mused, 'I haven't checked the gallery. Do you suppose they broke in there as well?'

He got up. 'Let's make sure.'

They did, but the spare key for the cottage was still in the drawer and nothing else was out of place.

On their way back, Kim said, 'You've been a brick. If you need to get back to your boat, go. I'll manage the police when they come.'

'No trouble. I was only doing maintenance work. It can wait.'

She laughed shakily. 'I just got back from London. You expect something like that to happen there, but in Dulsworth?'

Byron leaned back and the chair creaked under his weight. 'You were away over the weekend? Tell me about it.'

Kim realized he was trying to distract her, but she obliged anyway. She didn't mention she'd gone to the art exhibition with Mark, just that she'd visited Shelley.

The arrival of a police car interrupted them. Two men bent their heads when they came in.

Kim told them what had happened and Byron nodded. They took notes and the detective in charge asked to see the box room. She took him upstairs.

He looked around and said, 'It wasn't a forced entry. Nothing else was stolen or damaged?'

'No, nothing that I've noticed.'

'These paintings were valuable?'

'One or two could fetch a couple of thousand. The others were all worth less. Some aren't worth more than the frames they're in.'

'Then the good ones will fetch a decent sum on the black market?'

She shrugged. 'I suppose so, if someone knows where to sell them, but that'd be risky, wouldn't it?'

'I don't want to disillusion you, but the chance of finding them is minimal. If they were famous paintings, people are careful when they decide to buy, but no one's likely to bother about lesser-known artists. It'll be impossible to recover them once they're fed into the system.'

'Oh botheration! I thought they were safer here than in the gallery.'

He tried to give her a little reassurance. 'Your insurance company will compensate you.'

Feeling silly, she replied, 'They weren't insured. I didn't know that they were worth anything until recently, and I don't think I would have insured them anyway. I planned to sell them off in the next couple of months.'

'Oh, I see. What puzzles me is why anyone would risk breaking into a cottage like this one, practically next to the main road. There's a risk they'd get spotted. We haven't had many burglaries recently either, and none like this. Have you checked your gallery?'

'Yes, we just went there. It's untouched, and my spare key is still where I put it.'

'Do you have any photos of the pictures?'

'Yes. I needed pictures for someone who valued them.'

'Perhaps you can give them to us, just in case. Who else has access to your house? Who knew about the pictures? It looks like an inside job to me.'

'My parents have a key and there's a spare one in the gallery, in case I lock myself out.'

'And who knew about the pictures besides you?'

'Audrey and Ben. They've worked in the gallery for donkey's years. They've nothing to do with it I'm sure. My parents; my sister; Adrian Calderwood, a local artist — all know, but I'd put my hand in the fire for all of them. I'm not sure if I mentioned it to Simon, the man who valued them up in London. I have his card. He works for auctioneers and wouldn't risk his job.'

The police officer made notes. 'You'd

be surprised what people do for money. Anyone else?'

'Mark Fraser and his assistant Gloria. Mark put me in touch with Simon. He owns an art gallery in Poole. He deals in modern paintings, nothing like the stolen ones.'

'But he has connections to the art world.'

Reluctantly, she admitted, 'Yes, I suppose so. But he'd never get mixed up in anything criminal. I hope you're not going to bother him?'

'We have to keep all options open. We'll follow any possibilities.'

Clearing her throat, she said, 'Mark wasn't here this weekend. He was in London. In fact, we were together yesterday evening. He's still there now.'

'I see. Of course, there's always the possibility that someone overheard, or repeated the knowledge without thinking about the consequences.'

She ran her hands through her hair and explained, 'I haven't had the gallery very long. I'm trying to find my feet.

The paintings had been ignored for donkey's years. What you haven't had, you can't really miss, can you?'

'We'll do our best. The people will be here soon to check for fingerprints, although I don't think they'll find much. Whoever did it was careful not to leave any evidence. How many were there exactly?'

'I'm not absolutely sure. Between fifteen and twenty.'

Downstairs, Byron was talking to the other policemen. The uniformed constable commented, 'It's strange that they only took paintings. Usually they pick up anything worthwhile. You have some nice stuff, like those brass candlesticks on the mantelpiece, those snuff boxes over there, and so on. They'd be easy to dispose of on the black market.'

Byron said, 'I thought that was strange too.'

The inspector nodded and said, 'If you'll give us the photos, we'll be on our way again.'

Kim ruffled through a drawer and

handed him the bundle of photos. He took them and shook her hand at the door. 'We'll be in touch.'

After they'd gone, Kim told Byron, 'It looks like there's little chance of me ever seeing the paintings again.'

Byron nodded. 'That's what I gathered too. Sorry. Are you all right now? I have to open the pub. My father's gone for supplies. Come with me and have a hot pie.'

She shook her head. 'No thanks. I'm okay now. I'm not hungry. I'll arrange to have the lock changed. I'll wedge a chair under the front door tonight. I doubt very much if anyone will come back to the same place twice. The detective said he hoped the fingerprints-people will be here soon. I'd better stay here.'

'Okay! You know where I am. If you scream, I'll come running.'

★ ★ ★

Later that afternoon Kim's heart skipped several beats when her cell phone rang and she recognized Mark's number on the display.

'Hello, Mark!'

'I wanted to hear if you got home okay.'

'Yes, thanks. No problems. And you?'

'Fine. I just got back.' There was a slight pause.' 'Oh damn! Someone just came in. I have to go, but I'll be in touch soon. Bye!'

'It's okay. Bye!' She hadn't told him about the break-in, but she hadn't had time to tell him anything.

★   ★   ★

A knock at the door announced Audrey's arrival. News spread fast and she'd heard about the burglary. Kim made them coffee and brought her up to date.

'Good heavens! Nothing like that has happened around here for years. Are you sure that you're all right? Would you like me to stay here tonight, or would you like to come and stay with us?'

Kim was touched by the offer. 'It's super of you to offer, but I'll be fine. No one will come back to the same place two nights running. Someone is coming to change the lock on the door tomorrow, and putting some on the windows while they're at it. It's all unwanted expense but I'll never sleep easily again otherwise.'

Audrey nodded. 'If it makes you safer, it's worth every penny.'

19

Next day, Kim was in the gallery deciding which pictures to change around. She saw Mark's car draw up outside and felt a warm glow. He got out and slammed the door loudly. When he came in, she noticed that his dark brows were drawn in a straight line. She guessed something was very wrong.

'Hello, Mark.' She felt a ripple of excitement inside and she smiled at him automatically, despite his grim expression.

He didn't give her an inkling of a smile or a greeting. His voice had a chilled edge to it. 'Why the hell did you send the police to my gallery?' With hardened features, he continued, 'Have you any idea what a police car outside my place, and a couple of police officers inside, does for my business? I was negotiating with an important customer when they arrived. He didn't stay long after he heard the police mentioning stolen paintings.'

She was numb. Trying to keep calm, she said, 'I presume you're talking about the effect of the burglary?' He glowered and his features hardened. 'When the police asked me who knew the pictures were in the cottage, I told them. I also listed Adrian, my parents, my sister, Ben and Audrey, and Simon.'

'Then they probably think I'm a prime suspect, seeing that I'm in the same kind of business. Why didn't you warn me? Perhaps I could have visited the station and kept them away from my place.'

With her colour mounting, she said, 'When I got back, the cottage had already been burgled. You phoned me later, remember? You didn't have any time to listen to me and you cut our conversation short because you had a customer. Was I supposed to force you to listen to me?'

'And I suppose you couldn't phone me later and tell me what was going on?'

His tone and patronizing behaviour began to infuriate her. 'I was busy with my own problems. I didn't realize I needed to report everything that happens in my life to you! I honestly didn't think about the negative side of the police visiting your gallery. I told them you were in London. I thought that would exclude you from any direct investigation.' His stern expression baffled her. What had she done wrong? 'I understand why you think a visit from the police is bad publicity, but they didn't stay long, did they?'

He studied her for a never-ending second. 'Long enough for me to lose an important customer! If that gets around it'll have a domino effect.'

Kim froze and felt the screams of frustration at the back of her throat. She'd given her heart to a man who didn't even care that she'd been burgled. She glowered at him and snapped, 'That's all that matters, isn't it — business, business, business and the loss of a prospective customer. Someone stole my pictures, damn you! I can't control what the police do. I gave them your name among all the others. I told them you had nothing to do with it. Perhaps I could have given due warning if we'd talked long enough, but we didn't. You were busy. You're always busy, and I had other things on my mind.'

He stood there looking tall and angry. His hands were in his pockets and his dark eyes and dark lashes only made her dizzy with longings even though she felt terribly annoyed with him.

'I didn't believe Gloria when she said that she thought you were self-centred and merely using my friendship for your own ends. Perhaps she was right.'

The effect of his words made her feel more vulnerable than she'd ever felt in her life before. How could she ever believe she liked him? How dare he suggest that she'd 'used' him? Her face paled in anger. She had enough control to keep her voice low, although her body was taut like a tight spring.

'Gloria's psychological skills match her intelligence. I've never taken advantage of your friendship. I've never asked you for a favour, and I've never made any demands on your time. If you think about it, you'll agree with that.'

He ignored her words and retorted, 'It took a lot of persuasion to convince my customer it was a routine police enquiry and that I wasn't running some kind of illegal organization.'

Exasperated, Kim said, 'Mark, have you heard about the North American Indian saying, 'You can't eat money'? Think about it! I didn't want to involve you or your precious gallery. Anyone who gets too close to you gets burnt by the fire of your ambition. You should sort out your priorities! What the hell is the point in having a lot of money if the rest of your life is empty?' He continued to watch her with a very cold expression. 'I don't know what you were like before your marriage went on the rocks, but you're clearly incapable of trusting anymore. No one is perfect. I'm not; neither are you. Have you given one honest thought to how I felt? The police asked me perfectly logical questions. I answered them as best I could. I didn't accuse anyone of anything. I only told them what they wanted to know. If you think I valued your friendship for some self-centred reason, then you're wrong, and Gloria is too. I often wondered why you were helpful but I presumed it was out of friendship. I wanted to believe I was your friend, because I liked you. Perhaps you're not such a nice person after all. You haven't uttered a word of sympathy about the burglary, just made unkind, unjustified remarks. I'd be grateful if you please close the door on your way out!'

The silence between them became unbearable. His angry eyes met her angry expression. She studied his firm features and the confident set of his shoulders. His eyes were blazing, but so were hers. He turned away abruptly and went out through the open doorway, slamming it behind him.

She heard him start the engine a couple of times before it came to life. It complained loudly before he set off.

She felt hurt. It was almost a physical ache. She stormed into the rear room and grabbed the back of one of the chairs. She was glad there was no likelihood of visitors anymore today. Vaguely, she noted that her hands were shaking. Mark's words had shocked her more than the the burglary. She knew it was because she loved him desperately. If you loved someone, it was the hardest thing in the world to face undeserved anger.

She swallowed the despair in her throat and filled the kettle. She stared unseeingly out of the window as she waited for it to whistle. In all probability, they would never now act normally with each other again. That twisted and turned inside her like a sharp knife. She made a mug of coffee and cradled it in her hands as she sat at the table. She gulped hard but tears escaped and slipped down her cheeks. It wasn't the end of the world. She only had to remember how he'd just behaved. It would help her forget him.

Finally, she gave in to compulsive sobs. Business was bad, her property had been stolen, and the only man she'd ever wanted thought she'd intentionally involved him in an investigation about theft. Perhaps she should admit defeat and leave Dulsworth. She wasn't sure what would happen if she did. Perhaps the proceeds from a sale would still go to Uncle Bill's chosen charities. She'd never felt more like running away, but she wouldn't throw in the towel. Common sense reasserted itself. She rubbed the tears from her face and blew her nose on a sheet of kitchen-paper. She wouldn't give in.

Mark wasn't a frequent visitor to the village, and she'd cope with the occasional meeting if they did. There was no reason they couldn't act like civilized adults. They'd argued and he'd avoid her in future, but she could live with that. She had no intention of ever visiting Poole if she could avoid it.

Kim swilled out her mug, picked up her keys, switched off the lights and turned the sign on the door. She left the shadowed building behind and hurried home. Once inside, she fixed the new safety locks, drew the curtains and sat down on the sofa. Thinking about what had happened, she mused that life was very disheartening.

★　★　★

She slept fitfully and felt washed out and listless. It was Audrey's day to cover the gallery in the afternoon. Kim had already planned to visit a local house-sale. Audrey arrived just before she set out.

'You're looking very pale. Something wrong?'

'No. I'm okay. The outcome of the burglary I expect.'

'Why don't you spoil yourself and drive into town and go shopping? I find that's always a pick-up!'

Kim laughed softly. 'I'm alright, honestly. There's no point in throwing money away on something I don't need. I'll go to that house-sale instead. Let's have a cuppa before I leave. I still have plenty of time.'

They sat at the table and Audrey told her about her teenage son who was staying out too late and not taking school seriously. Kim listened with half an ear but she did pull herself together long enough to make suitable comments.

* * *

Kim drove along the narrow lanes towards her destination, and lowered the car window to let the cool air clear her brain.

The house was crowded. Lots of

people were wandering around, viewing things, picking them up and putting them down again. The auctioneers had sorted everything into categories. There were only a handful of pictures and paintings. One was a darkened village pond and a herd of cows painted in oils. Another depicted a picturesque cottage and a girl with a basket on her hips. Kim noted the lot numbers and joined the other people inspecting the rest of the items on offer.

She noted a set of willow-pattern dessert plates too. Shelley had a Welsh dresser and was searching for old willow-pattern dishes. They'd make a nice Christmas present. She suddenly realized that although she was thoroughly miserable, life went on, and she was still able to think about other things and other people.

She got both of the paintings for a very reasonable price. Someone else outbid her on the dishes. Only one other person had been interested in the paintings. After making a couple of half-hearted bids for one of the paintings, he'd lost interest.

Feeling satisfied with her day's work, Kim stopped on the way back for a hot pie and a cup of tea at a roadside cafe. She realized she hadn't eaten anything since breakfast the previous day, and the pie tasted good. Life went on.

She popped into the gallery on her way to the cottage. Audrey said, 'And? Bought anything?'

'Two smallish paintings. They're still in the boot of the car. I'll see if I can find out anything about the artists on the internet tonight. Any customers?'

'One couple came in. They were interested in that watercolour of the chasm. They wanted to think about it. They're staying with relatives near Lulworth, so there's a chance they'll come back.'

'Well that's better than nothing. If you need me for anything I'll be at home.'

Audrey nodded. 'Oh, Mark called in.'

Kim's heart stopped beating. Her

voice was unsteady and she hoped Audrey didn't notice. 'What did he want?'

'To talk to you, but he left a note instead. It's on the table in the kitchen.'

She walked through to the back room looking quite calm and picked up the envelope. Out of Audrey's sight, she ripped it open. She hated herself for how much a piece of paper from him meant to her. It contained a small sheet of paper from a notebook. The message was brief.

'I'm sorry I was unnecessarily angry yesterday. Please accept my apologies. — Mark.'

She stared at the solid dark writing. It was an apology, but it didn't contain a single really affable word or say they should forget it and move on. It was a businesslike statement — short and to the point. She bit her lip and stuffed it swiftly into her shoulder bag. Hurrying back through the shop, she called out, 'Bye!'

'Bye!' Audrey didn't look up from

where she was watering a potted plant in one of the corners.

Going next door, the wind buffeted Kim's body and she acknowledged that she couldn't turn love on and off, especially the kind of love she felt for Mark. It was a once-in-a-lifetime feeling. If he could show he didn't care, then she'd try to do the same. She clearly cared more about him than he did about her.

20

Kim's family was shocked when they heard about the robbery. She avoided telling them for a few days because she knew her dad would want to jump straight into the car and come down. He still vowed to make a detailed safety check of the whole place next time they came.

Shelley phoned and told her that they'd found out why she'd been unable to conceive. She explained the medical situation in detail. Kim grasped it had something to do with her fallopian tubes. An uncomplicated operation would sort it out and then they could look forward to becoming parents soon.

This development settled where the family would celebrate Christmas. Kim suggested they come to Dulsworth. She had enough room, and they all agreed. She started to make lists of what to do and what to buy.

Ella and Tom persuaded Kim to join the carol singers. As Christmas neared, they practised regularly in the village hall. It was fun to be part of the group and Kim was glad to get out of the cottage. When she was alone, her thoughts often circled around why things had gone wrong between her and Mark.

*   *   *

Winter winds blew fiercely. They whipped the grey sea into sharp waves, and made the boats bob about like little corks in the water. The garden had gone to sleep for the winter. A dark green holly tree with some bright red berries and hardy evergreen bushes were the only splashes of colour.

Christmas cards began to arrive and Kim sent her own. She brooded over whether to send Mark one, or not. In the end, she did. She just signed it without adding an extra message. A few days later one came signed from Mark. If he was still annoyed with her, two could play that game. She couldn't stop loving him but she didn't need to show it.

She was tempted to place his card on the mantelpiece among the ones from relatives and special friends. In the end, she hung it on one of the long red ribbons dangling down the side of the fireplace. She glanced at it too often. She missed his face and his presence.

One card from a friend in her former workplace puzzled her. Jenna had included a written a message on the side asking her how she felt about Howard's joke.

She invited Adrian to join them on Christmas Day. She thought he might be alone, but he was visiting his parents until after the New Year. He also said he'd almost finished her portrait. She could take a look any time after he got back.

On the last Saturday before Christmas, the carol singers arranged to sing outside the pub down by the harbour.

Dressed warmly, the group was in high spirits. At first just a handful of people listened, mostly friends and relatives. Gradually other people joined them. They'd already sung several carols by the time Byron came out of the pub with a tray of steaming punch. There was laughter and comments whilst the singers strengthened their voices. It was very cold. Kim looked at the small audience of people and discovered she knew most of them by name. Enjoying the mug of punch cradled between her gloved hands, she felt she belonged here. She was also extremely glad she was wearing thick woollen tights under her trousers and a warm bobble hat on her head.

Her heart flipped over when she noticed Mark standing at the back of the crowd. He was next to his car parked alongside the road. Kim's pulse accelerated as their glance met. He nodded but she was too startled to do anything but stare. She wasn't surprised to find her feelings hadn't changed. Her insides were in pandemonium. She wanted to belong to a man who didn't want her. He'd made that plain enough. She looked away and pretended to listen to someone's chatter.

When the conductor gathered them together again, Kim resisted looking in his direction. When she did, her heart plummeted when she saw he'd disappeared.

Loud clapping echoed as each carol ended. Their conductor encouraged the crowd to join in, and they all sang the final ones together. Mark's disappearance had saddened Kim but it had been a great evening. They were engaged to sing in the church on Christmas Eve and someone joked that at least the church wouldn't be so damned cold as it was here tonight.

★   ★   ★

Kim considered closing the gallery completely over the holiday season, but in the end she was glad she didn't. Four customers bought pictures during the week before Christmas. Her mum and dad arrived ahead of Roger and Shelley. Roger couldn't get away early. Numerous people always swamped the bookshop on Christmas Eve because they'd run out of any other ideas. When her parents arrived, she began to feel Christmas was happening at last. Kim had missed them. Her family was just what she needed to cheer her up at the moment.

She and her mother finished the shopping, pre-cooking and decorating. They were glad that the roads remained clear of snow, although they were very busy. Shelley and Roger arrived after eight on Christmas Eve. During the meal, everyone caught up on each other's news. They decided it would be a perfect start to the festivities to go with Kim to the midnight service at church.

Walking up the hill to the old building, they felt the first snowflakes on their faces and everyone agreed that nothing could be more perfect. Embedded in the surrounding darkness, the small village below them looked like a scene from a Christmas card. Lighted windows threw golden beams onto the cobbled streets and some people had decorated their house or garden with coloured lights. The church was already full when they arrived and Kim left her family to find a suitable place among the other carol singers near the front. The church looked wonderful with pots of large red poinsettias and firs decorating the stone altar and all the window niches. Candles burned brightly and a crib with its figures had a prominent position.

The vicar conducted the service with his usual verve. Finally, he invited the congregation to join the carol singers when they sang 'O Come All Ye Faithful', and it sounded like everyone did. Looking at the congregation, Kim was certain she'd done the right thing to move to this small village.

She was taken aback when she saw Mark among the crowd at the back. Her delight on seeing him tonight spread like a genial glow through her insides. She'd never feel the same love for anyone else ever again. He was all she ever wanted, and would never have.

After the last chords of the organ had died away, everyone shuffled outside and began to disperse. Some stood in groups to wish friends or relations a happy Christmas before they left. She went to search for her parents and her sister. They weren't alone and her step faltered for a moment when she saw them talking to Mark and a middle-aged couple.

Shelley looked up. 'Ah, here's Kim! Look, I just met Mark.'

Kim nodded dumbly and then managed to utter, 'Hello Mark.'

'Hello!' He turned to the people at his side. 'Mum, Dad, this is Kim. I told you about her. She moved to Dulsworth a couple of months ago and is running Bill's shop.'

A tall grey-haired man with a scotch-plaid scarf wrapped tightly round his throat held out his hand. 'Hello, Kim.

Well sung! Bill was a nice chap. He was a bit of an institution in the village. Always ready with a helping hand and an open mind.'

The colour rose in Kim's cheeks and nodded. 'Uncle Bill is a tough act to follow, but I hope that he knows I'm trying hard.'

He nodded. 'From what I hear, you'll make it. The atmosphere in church was very uplifting, wasn't it?'

'There's nothing quite like a church service on Christmas Eve, is there?'

His mother smiled at her. She was elegant: a well-dressed, slender woman in a soft camel-hair coat with a bushy fur collar rippling in the wind. Kim wondered if the fur was real; you couldn't tell these days.

Mrs. Fraser said softly, 'I love this church. It's full of memories for us. Do you like living here?'

Trying to avoid Mark's presence, Kim replied, 'Yes. I used to live in a much bigger town, but I feel very much at home here now.'

'Well you seem to already be fully integrated.' She smiled at Kim's family. 'I expect it's very special for you to have your family here for Christmas?'

'Yes, it's lovely,' Shelley replied.

Someone shouted 'Merry Christmas, Kim' and she waved without recognizing the voice. She looked down at Mark's polished shoes dotted with snowflakes. When she looked up, he was staring at her. She had a lump in her throat and wished she felt stronger. Strong enough not to feel he was special.

Turning to Kim's mother, Mrs. Fraser asked her where they came from and the two women chatted. The words drifted over Kim's head and she was almost glad when Shelley tugged her sleeve. Her parents smiled at Mark and said their goodbyes before they set off.

Shelley said, 'We've got to go, love. Mum put meat in the oven before we came out, and she's getting worried.'

Kim smiled. 'I set the automatic controls just in case.' She glanced at her watch in the sparse light. 'We've plenty of time, but we'll keep Mum happy.' She turned to Mark and his parents, smiled and said, 'Merry Christmas!'

His father said, 'Merry Christmas! It was a pleasure to meet you Kim.'

'Nice to meet you too. Bye!' She turned away.

She heard Mark's soft 'Merry Christmas' echo over her shoulder. Shelley hooked her arm through Kim's and they caught up with their parents and Roger, waiting by the church gate.

★   ★   ★

As soon as Mark and his parents were out of hearing, Shelley asked. 'What's up? I thought you two were making out.'

Kim looked steadily ahead. 'Really?'

'I thought you were really suited. He's refined and out of the ordinary.'

'You're right about that; but we're not suited.'

'What happened?'

'Nothing special. We had an argument — something to do with business.'

'Oh, I noticed the chill in the air. What was it about?'

'Nothing important. Let's enjoy Christmas. I don't want to talk about petty quarrels. Tell me what the doctor said. I presume there's nothing stopping you getting pregnant now, is there?'

Sidetracked, Shelley began relating and telling her how she was concentrating on getting pregnant.

21

Once Christmas was over and everyone had gone, Kim felt the loss. She'd loved having the family with her. Now things were settling back into the normal routine, she had too much time on her hands.

Ella invited Kim to join a crowd of others to her cottage on New Year's Eve. Kim pretended she was going home. She didn't feel like celebrating. Ella lived just outside the village so it was unlikely that she'd notice Kim was at home, alone. The New Year held no special promise and she preferred to be on her own. Her parents and Shelley presumed she was with friends, and she didn't disillusion them either.

She read that a local charity collected Christmas cards. Kim decided to take the decorations down and got a large envelope ready for the cards. When it came to Mark's card, she put it aside, although she knew she was being silly.

★   ★   ★

She read the cards again before she stuck them into the waiting envelope. When she reached the card from Jenna, she read about 'Howard and his joke' again. What did she mean? She found Jenna's telephone number and rang.

'Jenna? It's me, Kim. I wanted to thank you for your card and wish you a Happy New Year.'

'Kim! Lovely to hear from you. Thanks for yours, and a Happy New Year to you too.'

'How are things?'

'Fine. Work is a drag, but I don't need to tell you about that, do I?'

Kim laughed. 'Not if everything is as it was. What did you mean about Howard and a joke, on your card?'

'Didn't he clear it?'

'Clear what?'

There was a moment's silence. 'You

know what Howard's like. He zooms in on a party like a homing pigeon. We had our Christmas do early, because a lot of people planned to go away over Christmas. Howard gate-crashed it, even though he didn't know anyone except me and Lynette.'

'That's typical! I don't know why I bothered with him.'

'Me neither. He's good company when he makes an effort, so no one minded too much. It was okay for a while, until he got maudlin. He prattled on about his rugby club, his sister, and then about other things. He mentioned you, and said he'd had his own back. I asked him what he meant.'

'And?'

'He giggled and sniggered and said he'd made a copy of your key and driven down one evening when he knew you weren't home and took some paintings.'

Kim nearly fell off the chair. 'What? I'll kill him! I can't find the right words. How could he be so infantile? I reported the burglary to the police. Why did he do it?'

'I asked him why. He said he wanted to teach you a lesson, because you'd dumped him and he wanted revenge. I told him to buy you a bunch of flowers and return them straight away. I gather that he hasn't?'

'I'm gobsmacked. No, I haven't heard from him.'

'He's so stupid, he's probably forgotten about them by now.'

Kim remembered how Audrey had mentioned that Howard had phoned the Friday she'd gone up to London. She hadn't phoned him back later to find out why. 'Did anyone else hear him say he'd taken the pictures?'

'Yes — Betty, Clive, and Jan from reception. We were standing together and I think the others thought he was pulling our legs. When Howard noticed he'd said too much, he shut up and moved away. What are you going to do?'

'I'm not sure yet. I'll have to do something. I don't intend to let him get away with it. Thanks for telling me.'

'If I'd realized he hadn't returned them, I'd have got in touch before now.'

'I'm just grateful that you told me. I'll let you know what I did. You must come and visit me sometime. I'd like to see you again.'

'Love to. Later on in the year perhaps, when it's a bit warmer?'

'Good idea. It's very cold here at the moment.'

'Do you still enjoy your independence? I envy you every Monday morning when Mr. Johnson comes in and starts complaining.'

Kim laughed. 'It's not all pleasure. I'm still struggling to make ends meet.'

'I'll keep my fingers crossed for you.'

'Thanks for telling me about Howard. He has a brain the size of a peanut. Take care of yourself and keep in touch!'

'I will. Bye!'

'Bye!'

★ ★ ★

If Howard had been within reach, she'd probably have hit him with the telephone.

She continued to pack away the cards and decorations. If she went to the police and told them, Howard would end up charged with burglary. Did she want to see him in court, in jail, and unemployed? She detested him but she wouldn't be responsible for that.

She decided to confront him. If he returned the paintings, she'd tell the police it had been a practical joke and she wouldn't press charges. He didn't deserve it, but she wouldn't be the one to wreck his life.

★　★　★

Kim asked Audrey to look after the gallery and drove up to meet Howard from work. She waited for him at the company's exit. He looked suitably surprised, and then donned a self-righteous expression because he probably thought she wanted him back.

'Well hello there! What a surprise!'

Trying to stay calm, Kim said, 'Yes, I expect it is.'

'Sorry, darling, but I haven't got time for you this evening. I already have a date. You should have phoned first.'

'I've come for my pictures. I hope you still have them?'

His mouth dropped open and his eyes widened. 'Pardon! What pictures?'

'Howard, don't play the innocent with me! People told me you took my pictures from my cottage.'

'Who told you?'

'It doesn't matter who. I called the police because I thought it was a straightforward burglary. If I tell them you took them, you'll be up to your neck in hot water. Your only hope is to give them back. If you do, I'll go to the police and tell them it was a joke. If you don't I'll tell them to charge you with breaking and entering.'

He swallowed hard, and even in the sparse lighting Kim could see his Adam's apple bobbing in his throat. He thrust his hands into his pockets and tried to look nonchalant. 'I meant to return them, but you know how busy everything is around Christmas. I had too many games scheduled for the week-ends and too much to do in the week. Time just slipped away.'

'Howard, I don't care anymore why. I don't even want to talk about why you stole them. I can guess. I want them back now and you can pray that they haven't been damaged by bad storage. A couple of them were quite valuable.'

'I can't sort it out now. I'm already late. I've got a date with Sandra.'

'I don't give a monkey's uncle if you've a date with Cameron Diaz! Either I am on my way home with those pictures within the next hour, or I'll go to the police.'

'Oh hell! It was only a bit of fun!'

'Fun? You have a warped idea of fun. It's about time you grew up. Howard, where are my pictures? Are we going to get them now, or not?'

He gave in without further comment.

She followed him to his garage and she waited until he'd loaded the pictures into the back of her car. He slammed the door of the boot and stamped off into the darkness without another word.

*   *   *

The police were more understanding than she expected. They asked her several times if she was sure that she didn't want to press charges. She was. She just hoped she'd never see Howard ever again.

*   *   *

A couple of days later Adrian called. He sounded excited and his eyes sparkled. 'Guess what? Mark has persuaded someone to exhibit my stuff in a small gallery in the West End.'

Kim was delighted for him. 'That's wonderful. I'm sure it'll be a resounding success. Mark must have pulled a few strings.'

He nodded. 'The chance I've always wanted.'

'Come and have a cup of tea and tell me all about it. When is it?'

He followed her into the back room and flopped into a chair. 'February. Mark promised to come one evening this week, to help me pick the canvasses. Then I'll pack them and hire a van to take them up to London.'

She gave him a mug of tea and pushed a plate of biscuits closer. 'It sounds exciting!'

'You'll come of course?'

'If I can. Let me know when.' She wanted to avoid Mark. She needed to think carefully whether to go or not.

He took a sip. 'What about your portrait? Don't you want to see it? I'm putting it into the show, so if you don't call this week, you'll be too late.'

'I'm going to a house sale tomorrow and won't be back till late. Wednesday I'm stuck in the gallery all day. I think I'll wait until I see it on the wall in London. It sounds like you have plenty to do without me invading and making comments you don't want to hear.'

He laughed. 'You're one of the few people I can stand for any length of time because you're always honest. Okay! If that's what you want, you'll see it in London. I wonder if you'll like it. It'll be too late once it's on the wall.'

'I promise I won't complain, even if I hate it. I'll save my critique until we meet later.'

She didn't ask Adrian about Mark. The less she knew the better.

★   ★   ★

The invite to the show duly arrived two weeks later. Kim saw Adrian and Mark at the end of the same week. They were talking to someone when she passed them.

Adrian shouted buoyantly, 'Hello Kim!'

Mark's head shot up and after a pause, and he echoed Adrian's words.

Kim managed a tremulous smile and

replied with, 'Hello, you two!' Her heart was beating too rapidly and she looked down to hide her confusion. She didn't slow down, or try to cut into the conversation. The sight of Mark gave her collywobbles.

Adrian glanced at them both and wondered what had gone wrong.

Kim went into the post office. When she came out, there was no sign of Mark or Adrian anymore. She went home by the back roads in case they were still around, and patted herself on the back. Mark never had many reasons to come to the village. She was now almost glad his house was further away.

22

As the date for Adrian's exhibition drew closer, Kim decided she had to go. He'd be very disappointed if she didn't, so she resigned herself to it. She arranged to stay with Shelley, and planned to return next day. The weather was picking up slightly and she looked forward to more tourists soon.

★　★　★

When Kim arrived in London, she could already tell by the brilliant look on her sister's face that she was pregnant. She hugged Shelley. 'You don't need to tell me. I can guess. You've done it! You're pregnant!'

Shelley dragged her inside and shut the door quickly. 'Yes, it's brilliant. I'm so excited.'

'How far?'

'Only a couple of weeks. I haven't been to the doctor's yet, but one of those self-test packs says I am. I'm feeling wonderful.'

'Do Mum and Dad know?'

'They know we'd like to have a family and they're delighted about that already.'

'When are you going to the doctor's for official confirmation?'

'I'll go in a week or two. I'll spend a fortune on over-the-counter tests until then.'

'I think they are pretty reliable these days. Clever girl! How about a cup of tea? Then you can tell me all.'

Shelley led the way into the kitchen. Kim felt a tinge of envy. Shelley had a great husband and was now founding a family. It would probably never happen to her. The only man she'd ever loved was out of reach. You dreamed about a family once you'd found the right person.

★ ★ ★

Next evening Shelley watched Kim dress. 'That's perfect. It's a lovely shade of grey. It shimmers and is just right for your colouring.'

Kim mused that it didn't really matter what she looked like. After she'd spoken to Adrian, she'd scoot. 'It's not new. I bought it for a friend's wedding last year.'

'Well, it's perfect for tonight.'

Kim went by taxi. Light spilled through the windows onto the pavement and she saw that the rooms were crowded. She added her coat to a bundle of others lying across a counter near the door and straightened her skirt before she entered the fray.

She wandered and studied the pictures. She already knew most of them and was smug in the knowledge. She noticed some of the pictures already had 'sold' signs on them and she felt happy for Adrian. It was an indication that people already appreciated his talent.

There was a group in front of Kim's

portrait. She stopped there longer than anywhere else. It was a very strange feeling to see oneself on the wall. Some people noticed the resemblance and whispered among themselves. He'd done a brilliant job of catching her with a wistful expression on her face.

Someone touched her arm. 'It's good, isn't it?'

She turned and saw Mark's friend Jeffrey. She smiled. 'Hi, Jeffrey! Yes, it is. I haven't seen it before. It's strange to see oneself like that.

He nodded and gestured around with his hands. 'The whole lot is very good. I think we'll hear a lot more of him in the future.'

'I hope so. He's talented, and a nice person into the bargain.' She noticed the 'sold' sign on the framework of her portrait. 'Oh look! Someone's already bought it. I suppose I should have offered for it, but someone probably paid more for it than I can afford at present.' She felt a little pensive about her likeness ending up in foreign hands.

'Where's Wanda?'

'Over there talking to some TV presenter. Come and say hello!'

She could hardly refuse; that would seem rude. She followed him.

Wanda was alone. She looked up and gave a lazy smile. 'How nice! You again! Jeffrey, be a love and get us something to drink.' She handed him her empty glass and Jeffrey went in search of the wine waiter. 'How are you and your gallery getting on?'

'I'm fine; the gallery is surviving! And you?'

'Can't complain! My feet are killing me because I bought a pair of shoes that are half a size too small. They looked too good and I got carried away.'

Kim eyed the red patent eye-catchers. 'I wouldn't mind a pair like that myself. They're quite something. Why don't you take them off for a bit? Give your feet a chance to recover. You're standing by the wall. No one will notice.'

Wanda grabbed her and kissed her cheek. 'You're right!' She eased her feet out of the shoes and sank by a couple of centimetres but looked happier. 'Oh God, that's wonderful! Where's Mark?'

Kim composed her expression. 'Haven't a clue. I haven't seen him. We aren't a twosome. I told you that before. I only came tonight because I know the artist and he wanted me to come.'

Wanda paused. 'Oh, I presumed you two were more than just friends by now. You're suited. I even told Jeffrey so'

Kim shook her head. 'We're too different.'

'I don't think so. Mark wasn't very happy for quite a time, but he's livened up a lot recently. I thought it was all thanks to you. I thought he'd found someone at last who understood him.'

Kim shrugged. She didn't intend to give anything away. 'I don't think I'm cut out to handle someone as complicated as Mark. The past weighs too heavily on him, and I'm not prepared to be second best.'

Wanda nodded. 'I can understand that. It isn't easy to get close to him, but you were good for him.'

'I'm not. He doesn't trust me.'

Wanda's eyebrows lifted. 'What does that mean?'

Kim shrugged dismissively. 'We had a quarrel about something trivial. He blamed me for something that was unimportant. He was positive it was all my fault and expected me to kow-tow. I didn't. When you start toeing the line just to keep the peace it gets you nowhere.'

Wanda nodded. 'Agreed! Jeffrey and I bicker sometimes about trivialities, but we agree about the important things. I know that people think that we're mismatched, but we have blind faith in each other and we've been together for more than ten years.'

Kim smiled. 'Then you're very well suited. How are your feet now?'

'Much better! Ah, here comes Jeffrey, and look who's with him.'

Following in Jeffrey's wake was Adrian and behind him was Mark.

Kim's stomach clenched. Adrian flung his arms around her and kissed her on the cheek. 'Hi, Kim. I wasn't sure if you'd come.'

She looked up into his laughing face. 'I couldn't stay away, could I? I wanted to be here on your first step to fame. I love the show; it's great! The first Adrian Calderwood exhibition! Congratulations.'

He grinned. 'Not quite. You held the first one.'

'Some of the paintings are new to me, but if I had a lot of money, I'd buy one of them. I notice my portrait has gone, but I couldn't have afforded it anyway.'

'Why didn't you tell me you wanted it? I would have given it to you.'

The tense lines on Kim's face had lessened a little by the time she turned to face Mark. 'Hello, Mark.'

He eyed her with an unreadable expression. 'Hello! How are you?'

'Fine, thanks.' She was glad to accept a glass of wine from Jeffrey. It gave her an excuse to look away again. She didn't want to study him. It hurt too much. Adressing Adrian, she said, 'I loved that picture of the green glass bowl I saw in your cottage, but it isn't here.'

He shrugged. 'I wanted to show a decent range of my stuff. There wasn't room for everything.'

She knew it was foolish to avoid Mark, but she needed to keep her feelings hidden. There were too many people who might notice the longing in her face. She looked across briefly when he chatted to Jeffrey. She reminded herself about his hostile attitude the day they'd quarrelled and the lack of contact since then. As long as she did that, she'd sail through the evening without any more problems.

Kim put her glass on a nearby shelf and tucked her arm through Adrian's 'Show me the rest of your pictures.'

It gave Adrian another chance to circulate and catch the occasional comment. They left the others and went on a tour of the room. Now and then, they stopped to look at a picture she hadn't seen before. Several times, visitors chatted to him when they realized that he was the artist. Kim could tell how much he relished the attention.

In a one of the quieter corners, he said, 'You can't fool me. What's wrong? You're so tense and nervous. You're normally so calm and collected.'

She thought she could tell him anything, but she couldn't talk to anyone about herself and Mark. 'Everything's okay. It's the effect of the city. I enjoy it for a while but I love more peaceful surroundings these days.' She wanted to talk about something else. 'Are you enjoying yourself this evening?' It worked.

He grinned. 'I'm delighted. I thought I'd never make it. I've you to thank for it, you and Mark.'

'This has nothing to do with me.' Kim swept around with a gesture of her hand. 'This is Mark's doing.'

'Ah! But you introduced me to Mark, didn't you?'

She laughed softly. 'And I'm glad I did.' She looked at her watch. 'I'm going to leave. I'm sure you'll stay until the last person leaves. I'm glad I came to be here on the night of all nights.' She kissed his cheek. 'Will you say cheerio to the others from me? We're near the entrance here. I'll see you when you get back home. Give me a call. Come for coffee and tell me all!'

Adrian looked at her thoughtfully again, but didn't try to stop her. He noticed the determination in her expression. 'Sure?'

She nodded. 'I'm catching an early train. I haven't had time for a chat with my sister yet. If I leave now, we can catch up on news before she goes to bed. Go back to the others and enjoy your fame!' She gave him a quick kiss on his cheek and left him. He watched her for a moment and then went to join the others.

Kim pulled her coat from beneath the pile and went out into the cold night air. She strolled in the direction of the next tube station. It had rained recently and the pavement mirrored the lamplight. She pulled up the collar of her coat and looked at her watch. It was still early. The tube was still comfortably busy and at the other end, it was an easy walk to Shelley's flat. The wet leaves tumbled around her high heels as the wind blew them hither and thither. Her footsteps echoed and she thought about the exhibition and Mark. She wasn't sorry she'd hardly spoken to him. She didn't know what they'd talk about anymore.

★   ★   ★

Next morning Kim was awake early. Roger had already gone and Shelley was just about to go. Shelley sat down at the breakfast bar. 'I still have a few minutes.' She nursed her half-empty coffee mug. 'What was it like last night? Enjoy yourself?'

Still in her pyjamas, Kim spread butter liberally on a slice of toast. 'It was good. Adrian's pictures are great. I'm not just saying that. I think he has a future in art. I met Wanda and Jeffrey again. They're nice, both of them.'

'And Mark?'

She attacked the toast. 'Yes. He was there.'

Shelley reached out and clasped her wrist. 'Hey! You can't kid me, I'm your big sister, remember? You like him a lot, don't you?'

Kim laid her knife aside and nodded. 'Yes, but we don't match, so stop building castles in the air.'

Shelley looked briefly at her watch again. She got up and grabbed her coat and bag from a nearby stool. 'I wish I could stay, but time's up. I've got to dash.' She pecked Kim's cheek.

'I'm fine. Don't worry!'

Shelley nodded. 'I'll be in touch!' She left in a flurry and Kim heard the door slam behind her.

Kim was determined to keep her misery bottled up inside. There was no point in loading her problems onto other people, not even onto her own sister.

23

Kim arrived in plenty of time to open the gallery that afternoon. There were no visitors but when she looked out of the window, she felt more optimistic. Crocuses and snowdrops were blooming at last, and the bushes and trees had fat buds.

*　*　*

Next morning the sky was grey again but the clouds had silver linings. The gallery was closed until after lunch. She could either do her ironing, or go for a walk. Kim opted for the fresh air. She dressed warmly because she could tell that the wind was cold. She often went for a walk along the top of the cliffs. Some days the sky was full of winter sunlight; other days it was dull and disagreeable. She always turned back long before she reached Mark's house. In the beginning, she didn't want him to think she was fishing for an invitation, and now she was avoiding him.

On her way through the village, she noted some people were already busy in their gardens. She climbed the steep path to join the coastal path. She met a man on his way home with his dog and the two of them exchanged friendly greetings. The wind whipped her scarf around her face. Kim thrust her hands deeper into her pockets.

She walked contentedly for a while. The wind chaffed at her face and her skin felt tight across her cheeks, but she was glad she'd come. She stopped now and then to gaze at the grey sea and watch the waves surging and crashing onto the rocks far below. A couple of ships were making slow progress far out to sea. They looked like toys bobbing on the water.

She'd been along the path numerous times since her arrival and she knew where to turn back to avoid Mark's house. Wiry grass and windswept gorse bushes lined the pathway and she'd gone far enough.

The wind howled in the crevices and the waves crashed onto the rocks below. She heard Mark call her name and she looked up. He was coming towards her. Kim clenched her hands into tight balls in her pockets and she waited until he reached her. She had to swallow a lump in her throat when she studied his familiar features.

The wind was trying to grab the ends of his scarf but it was stuffed securely inside his thick jacket. He clearly hadn't reckoned with meeting her here. His voice was hesitant. 'I was just coming to see you.'

'Really? I'm on my way home.'

He nodded absentmindedly and said, 'We need to talk. You left before I had a chance yesterday.'

Kim refused to stand and look at him. Without commenting, she turned away and began to walk homeward again. He fell into step. She kept her head down and stayed out of reach.

'Adrian had an interview with an art critic last night and I'd promised to support him. I only got home a couple of minutes ago.'

She was glad to see the rooftops of the first straggling houses on the edge of the village coming into sight. She decided to get it over with and deal with whatever he wanted. 'What do you want to talk about?' Her throat was dry and she ran her tongue over her lips.

'Us!'

She flinched and her expression tightened. 'We haven't much to talk about, have we? I wonder if we ever did. Our last real conversation ended quite brilliantly. It made me realize how little we empathized. There's no point in talking, unless it's to do with business.'

He came to a halt and she stopped to face him. 'Kim, I know I was brainless and very stupid. I said what I said that day deliberately.'

She drew a deep breath and stared at

him. 'Deliberately? What do you mean, deliberately?'

'I wasn't blind to what was happening between us. I decided to torpedo our friendship before it got out of control. I thought it was better that way.'

'Better for who, you or me?'

He looked ill at ease. 'I vowed not to let another woman control me emotionally again. I used the police calling at my gallery that day as an excuse to erect a barrier between us.'

Kim felt her chest tighten and tears gathered at the back of her eyes. She looked out to sea. 'Well, you must be pleased. You were very successful.'

He shifted and ran his hands through his hair. 'I'm so sorry! I didn't want to hurt you, but I thought I was doing the right thing because I didn't want our relationship to intensify. I regretted every single word later and I was unhappier than I've ever been in my life before. I presumed things would calm down and we'd remain friends. I now realize it was already too late for that. You meant too much to me.'

She listened and concentrated on the sight of the stormy grey sea. She dragged her gaze away and back to his face. She swallowed hard. 'What do you expect me to say? That I understand? That I don't mind? I can't do that, because I don't understand, and I do mind. I hadn't done anything to warrant your anger that day. Why didn't you just tell me to push off and ignore you? I'm not stupid.'

'I don't like lying and I lacked the guts to tell you I wanted to stay clear of you.'

Kim drew a deep breath and hoped her voice didn't shake. 'I don't believe that. You could have wrapped the message up nicely in the right words. I'd have understood, without the theatricals. I never tried to trap you into anything. I wasn't looking for an affair or anything more permanent. I was happy with my life as it was until we met.'

His voice was pleading. 'From the

very first time I kissed you, I knew you were special. My interest grew ceaselessly until I felt I'd lost complete control. I found myself thinking about you day and night.'

She tried to keep the sarcasm out of her voice. 'So you pushed me away. People meet, and people like each other. Sometimes they stay together; sometimes they drift apart again. You didn't even give us a chance.'

'I didn't want to hurt you, Kim. I thought it would be easier for you, as well as for me, if we didn't fall in love.'

She turned abruptly, unwilling to listen to any more. She was about to walk on. He took her arm. 'Wait, Kim! Please don't go, not yet!'

Her eyes blazed and she said heatedly, 'We have nothing to talk about. I don't understand you, but I'm not sure if it matters anymore. You want us to be casual friends? Okay, let's go our own separate ways from now on.'

The wind whistled around their faces and the sea crashed somewhere on the rocks far below. 'I now realize that's not what I want at all,' he said. 'I don't want a platonic friendship. I'm asking you to give me another chance.'

'Why should I?'

'Only one reason.'

'And that is?'

'I love you. I think I have done so from the start. I know I acted like an idiot and I don't deserve it, but I'm asking you to forgive me.'

Her tongue felt dry in her mouth and she stared at him wide-eyed.

'I think my reaction was rooted in my failed marriage. I didn't want to face anything like that ever again and I've continued to wonder how much I was to blame.'

'Mark, your wife is part of your past but she's not part of mine. I've no intention of fighting a ghost. If you think all women are the same, you'll never be able to trust me, or any other woman either.'

'I do trust you, and I want you more than I ever thought I'd want anyone again. The more I thought about you, the more I realized I'd been a bloody fool not to explain what I felt. I was afraid to talk about the past.' He continued in a pleading tone. 'Kim, I was scared of opening myself to you; of being rejected.'

There were tears hovering at the back of her eyes but somehow she kept them in check. She hoped her voice didn't give her away. 'I can live with your past because it has nothing to do with me, but if you shut me out of your problems, no matter what they are, it won't work. I never wanted more than you were willing to give. I was just glad to be your friend. You need more than friendship when you love someone — you need complete and everlasting trust.'

He nodded. 'I know. My attitude has nothing to do with you. I stopped loving Jill a long time before I applied for a divorce. After she drowned I wanted to move on but her memory got in the way and my doubts remained.'

He looked helpless. She wanted to take him in her arms but she did nothing and she floundered in mid-air.

He continued, 'I was rotten to you that day, but I told myself it was for your own good. I've always wondered if the breakdown of my marriage was more my fault than Jill's. I didn't want to put you, or myself, through anything like that again.'

Kim said slowly, searching for the right words, 'Don't you think you could have explained and given us a chance? Your wife cheated on you with someone else and the accident wasn't your fault. You weren't to blame, and you know it.'

He looked bleak, but he nodded. The wind was calm for a moment. His expression lightened and his voice hushed to a whisper. 'I had the feeling we belonged together almost from the first day we met but I didn't want to saddle you with my past. I love you, Kim, and I want us to be together always. Forgive me for pushing you away. You're the other half I always hoped to find. I don't want to bulldoze you into anything, but please give me another chance!'

He looked at her with longing and touched her cheek. Her defences began to crumble and her heart turned over in response. He was all she ever wanted. A prickle of excitement fretted her skin and there was a tingling in the pit of her stomach.

She nodded, and her voice shook a little. 'Promise never to shut me out ever again?'

'I promise!' He looked out to sea for a moment but then he sounded more confident. 'When I met Jill, I was young, impressionable, and thought it was love, but it wasn't. I enjoyed having someone decorative on my arm, and she liked the kind of comfortable lifestyle I provided, but the rest was shallow and artificial. We drifted apart because nothing held us together. I didn't believe in real love anymore until I met you. You're beautiful, intelligent, and caring. I'm at peace with you. I want you, and I want to be there for you, for the rest of my life.'

He groaned and pulled her into his arms. His mouth covered hers hungrily. It sent the pit of her stomach into a wild whirl. His lips covered hers again and then he looked up and said, 'I don't care about the past anymore. I've figured out that only here and now matters. I want you to love me.'

The tension slipped away as she studied his face. Locked within the protection of his arms, she felt the strength of his body. She wanted to be there for him always, in good times and bad. He kissed her again and it left her feeling weak and euphoric. He smiled and the relief in his face made him look young and carefree.

'I love you more than I can express.' He stared at the stormy clouds and then grinned. 'Can we finish this conversation somewhere that's more comfortable? We don't have to stand in the middle of a force-ten gale, do we? My house is closer than yours is. Come back with me and let's make up for lost time.' He looked at her earnestly. 'Can you love a very stupid man, after what's happened?'

She nodded silently. 'I love you a lot, you idiot!'

'Thank heavens!' He swung her around and set her gently on her feet again.

'Mark, I have to open the gallery in an hour's time.'

His eyes twinkled. 'You can give it a miss today, can't you? There's not much hope anyone will turn up on a windy February afternoon.' He tipped his head to the side. 'If you insist, I'll come with you.'

She smiled. 'No, you're right.'

He threw back his head and laughed. 'Perhaps, if you're good and promise to stay a while, I'll show you the hidden tunnel.'

'That's bribery!'

'I'll use any means to keep you at my side. I intend to tempt you into sharing the rest of your life with me.'

She nodded silently. 'You don't need

to tempt me. I'm yours already.'

He lifted her hand to his lips. 'Come and see the house. I hope you'll like it. If not, we'll sell it and buy something else. Come and see Adrian's portrait above the mantelpiece.'

Her insides whirling and catching her breath, she said. 'My portrait?' Her mouth opened slightly and he kissed her quickly again.

'You don't think I'd let him sell the portrait of the woman I love to some idiot who wouldn't appreciate it, did you?'

Her body ached for his touch and the prospect of being alone with him at last was wonderful and it made her breathless. They were travelling side-by-side down the same road at last. 'I hope you don't think you can tell me how to run my gallery?'

He threw back his head and laughed deeply. Putting his arm around her waist, he drew her closer. 'I promise that I'll never interfere. I'll keep my mouth shut and my thoughts to myself unless you ask for my advice. Your gallery is yours, mine is mine, and never the two shall meet — unless of course you manage to find another Adrian!'

He reached out for her hand and she slipped hers into his, feeling the warmth and the safety. He held it tight. 'I love you. I'll never stop loving you, Kim. I know my life will have a real purpose at last. I'm planning to make you happy.'

His words set her heart pounding. She nodded. 'I love you too. I have for weeks and weeks.' Reaching up, she kissed him, and he looked at her with dreamy intimacy before he reclaimed her lips and crushed her to him. She felt utter delight. He was a man who was full of twists and turns, but she loved him. She wanted no other.

They went towards the mullioned house. Weak rays of sunshine reflected in the windows. The old building was waiting to welcome them. He held her tightly and they shared moments of sheer delight. He was the forever-kind-of-man she'd always hoped to find.

They were ready to face the storms of life, all its struggles and its rewards. They had time. They had love, and future prospects were wonderful — better than either of them had ever expected just a few short weeks ago.

THE END

We do hope that you have enjoyed reading this large print book.

Did you know that all of our titles are available for purchase?

We publish a wide range of high quality large print books including:
Romances, Mysteries, Classics
General Fiction
Non Fiction and Westerns

Special interest titles available in large print are:
The Little Oxford Dictionary
Music Book, Song Book
Hymn Book, Service Book

Also available from us courtesy of Oxford University Press:
Young Readers' Dictionary
(large print edition)
Young Readers' Thesaurus
(large print edition)

For further information or a free brochure, please contact us at:
Ulverscroft Large Print Books Ltd.,
The Green, Bradgate Road, Anstey,
Leicester, LE7 7FU, England.
Tel: (00 44) **0116 236 4325**
Fax: (00 44) **0116 234 0205**

THE HOUSE ON THE HILL

Miranda Barnes

When a young man moves into the old house next door, Kate Jackson's curiosity is piqued. However, handsome Elek Costas is suspiciously reclusive, and the two get off to a bad start when he accuses her of trespassing. Whilst Kate is dubious of Elek's claim to be the rightful owner, her boyfriend Robert has his eye on acquiring the property for himself . . . Just what is the mystery of Hillside House? Kate is determined to find out!